I0619867

THE BINDING

Unexpected Magic #1

SAMANTHA JACOBEY

Lavish Publishing LLC

Unexpected Magic #1

First Edition

All Rights Reserved

Published in the United States by Lavish Publishing, LLC, Midland, Texas

Paperback edition

ISBN: 9781944985103

Cover Design by: Wycked Ink

Cover Images: Adobe Stock

www.LavishPublishing.com

Contents

Prologue

LIFTING THE BOOK ANXIOUSLY, Ezamay caressed the leather binding. Her fingers trembled slightly as she traced the outline of a long, slender object hidden inside it. Satisfied that it wouldn't be noticed, she replaced the text on the table and searched for her phone in her pocket.

Fishing out the device, she dialed the number from memory, not daring to store it in her cell. "Teddy? It's time," she whispered hoarsely.

"Is it arranged?" a deep male voice inquired.

"Yes," Ezamay replied a bit more confidently. "Everything's in place, or will be by the end of the day. Garrett will contact you once things are in motion."

"Very well. I'll be ready."

Dead air followed, and she knew he had hung up. Darkening her screen, she stared at her phone for a long moment before she returned it to her sweater's oversized pouch. "Glenda!" she called loudly.

"Yes, ma'am." The housemaid entered through the tall arch that connected the foyer to the study, smoothing her apron over her uniform skirt.

"We will need a tea service as soon as Meri arrives," Ezamay informed her stiffly. "Be sure to include those little cakes that she likes so much."

"Yes, ma'am." Glenda nodded as she backed out of the room.

Turning to the window, Ezamay watched the large oak tree outside sway in the afternoon breeze. Her thoughts on the past, she sighed deeply, recalling the days when she had lived in a more modest dwelling, without servants to cater to her every whim. *Seems so long ago,* she lamented.

For twenty-five years, she had been the matron of the Monroe residence. She had married Garrett in one year and given birth to their only child the next, and in all the time since, she had kept her former life hidden. None knew of her childhood, nor did they suspect her secrets.

Time had grown short since Merideth had graduated from college a year ago. *Damn her,* Ezamay cursed her daughter under her breath. Immediately, she cringed, well aware that the situation was not her daughter's doing. Her eyes narrowed, she glared at the dancing limbs. *This is my fault; and I'm the one who has to fix it.*

A sleek black Mercedes pulled into the drive, and a tall, slender young woman stepped out, causing Ezamay to catch her breath. An ache formed in the pit of her gut as she watched her close the door to her vehicle and glide towards the entrance. Waiting patiently, Meri joined her a moment later.

"Hello, Mother," Merideth used a soft voice when addressing her.

"Hello, darling," Ezamay replied, turning to give her visitor a half hug. "How was your journey?"

"Relaxing." Meri smiled. "It's good to be home for a visit, even one as short as this."

"Indeed." Ezamay indicated the couch as Glenda returned with a silver tray filled with cups, plates, pastries, and a pot of fresh tea. "I'm glad you could make it," she said lightly, lifting the tome and placing it on the end table that sat where the chair and sofa formed a corner. "I have a gift for you."

Eyeing the large leather-covered text, Meri's lips curled. "Another old book?"

"Yes." Ezamay's eyes sparkled. "A very old one passed down through my family from mother to daughter, one generation to the next."

Merideth struggled to hold her grin, only half succeeding. "You didn't ask me here for another lecture, did you?" she asked stiffly.

"No." Her mother shook her head, her hand resting lightly on a worn edge of her offering. "I understand your choice. Having a family is a big decision, and first you must meet the right man."

"Mother," Meri breathed, her smile gone, "I told you. I like my freedom. I don't need a man to complete me! Why can't you just accept that I'm happy with my life the way that it is?"

A tear glinted in the older woman's soft blue orb, and she blinked rapidly to remove it. "No lecture, sweetheart. I understand your choice. I respect it. I only give this to you that you may read it if you wish. It is a diary, of sorts, with each woman adding a bit of her own story before passing it along. My pages are at the end, with a few blank ones left for your story. Yours will be the last that will be added." She sniffed.

Shaking her head, Meri poured herself a cup of tea and dropped in a spoon full of sugar. "Thank you, Mother," she said as politely as she could muster. Taking a sip, she envisioned the shelf in her New York flat that held the rest of her mother's treasures. This newest addition would join them, and some day, she might actually take the time to peek inside it.

ONE

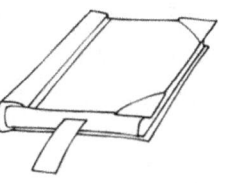

Guardian

"DO you think we should be doing this?" Rider asked, turning only slightly towards the older man to his right.

"We don't have a choice," the other man replied, keeping his voice equally low.

Staring at the girl facing him, Rider's pulse quickened. Watching her dab at her eyes and occasionally wipe under her nose, he knew her pain. "It doesn't feel right," he insisted. "Maybe we could—"

"No, we can't," his father cut him off, his tone a bit gruff this time. "Until we get some answers, this is how it has to be."

A slight drizzle dripped down on them, turning into a heavy sprinkle and eventually a downpour. Adjusting his umbrella over his head, the younger man sighed deeply. No longer able to hear the priest's words due to the deluge drumming the taught cloth above him, he focused on the gathering. His eyes roving over the mourners, he knew the odds were good that one of them was a murderer.

"Do you know any of these people?" he asked a bit louder to beat the noise of the rain.

"Some." Thaddeus Bradshaw's steel grey eyes also searched.

Rider's matching blue orbs narrowed into slits as he watched a heavy-set man work his way through the crowd, stopping when he stood directly behind Merideth.

"Dad," he growled, "on her six."

"That's her uncle," his father informed him.

"Are you sure?"

"Yes. I've known this family since I was a child." the senior Bradshaw shifted to peek around to the sides and behind them. "We grew up on the same block, back when neighbors knew each other."

"Then why is this the first time I've heard of them?" Rider adjusted his long jacket against the dropping temperatures. "Damn. I think they're going to get an early winter here."

"Maybe. Virginia can be fickle like that." Thad nudged the arm next to him. "I think it's over."

"You haven't answered my question," Rider prodded as they joined the line to walk by the casket. His heart beating rapidly inside his chest, he covertly blew air into his palms and sniffed it. *If I'm going to meet this girl, the least I can do is make a good impression.*

Ignoring him, Thaddeus reached for the grieving widower's hand. "Garrett, I'm sure sorry about your loss."

Watching Meri over the tops of their arms, Rider recognized the sullen expression. Her eyes red and swollen, her thick layer of makeup could not mask her sorrow.

Stepping forward, he offered to shake as well. "Mr. Monroe."

"Hi, Rider. I've heard so much about you," Garrett said politely.

"Oh? From whom?"

Laughing anxiously, the two older men exchanged a glance before the shorter man clamped his arm around the girl's shoulders, hugging her against him in a half embrace.

"Gentlemen, this is my daughter, Merideth."

"How do you do?" Rider offered her his digits, regretting it a moment later when she gave him a dead-fish shake. Forcing a smile, he made the offer, "Can we take the two of you to dinner?" He had been rehearsing the line all morning and, having finally said it, felt as if a weight had been lifted off his chest.

"I'm afraid we can't." Garrett shook his head. "We have a large amount of family here at the moment. But they'll be leaving in the morning. Perhaps tomorrow night we can get together and catch up?"

"Sounds wonderful." Thad nodded on the agreement. "We'll get a reservation for us at six at Joshua Wilton House."

His mention of her favorite restaurant caught the girl's

attention for a brief moment, his smile seeming out of place when she glanced at him before purposely looking away.

Staring at the creased skin around the clear blue orbs of the younger man, Meri guessed him to be at least thirty. Blinking at him a few times, her eyes burned from the hours she'd spent crying.

She had just buried her mother, and the last thing she wanted to do was to be sociable. Only half listening as they arranged for an evening together, she thought about the last time she had seen her mother alive.

She had made the trip home only a few weeks before. Her mother had grown temperamental during the last year, since Meri's graduation from UCLA. She had thought finishing and moving to New York and closer to home would settle the older woman's attitude, but it hadn't.

They had shared tea and spent a few hours visiting, but the conversation constantly returned to their latest point of contention.

Merideth had informed her mother nine months ago, when she accepted the position at Muriel Brandolini, Inc., that there would be no grandchildren to dote over. Her mother had taken every opportunity since to make her feel guilty about the choice and to try to persuade her otherwise.

Shaking off the dark thoughts, Meri turned to the man who stood next to her, noting that he studied her intently. "I'm sorry," her voice cracked. "I'm ready to go back to the car."

"I'll walk you," he informed her, leaving the two older men to greet the rest of the mourners. Offering her his arm, he waited patiently for her to take it.

Stealing glances at him as they picked their way through the puddles, she leaned slightly against him to stay beneath the umbrella that he held between them.

The rain had only added to the sadness of the occasion, in her mind suiting it perfectly.

Arriving at the car, she noted that he had a ponytail formed by dark ringlets that hung a few inches down his back. "Thank you... Rider, was it?" she said softly as he helped her into the car.

"Yes." He grinned, giving her a small nod. "Would you like for me to join you until Mr. Monroe arrives?"

"No. I'll be fine." She shook her long, honey-colored strands and settled into the leather-covered seat. "My father will be here when everyone is gone." Staring straight ahead, she dismissed the stranger.

"All right," he agreed. "I'll see you tomorrow evening." Closing the door firmly, he adjusted his umbrella to better block the spray as he returned to the older men as the last of the line filed past.

Shaking hands again, the three men said their goodbyes. Garrett trudged towards the long black limo that would carry them home, while Rider and Thad strode through the wet grass.

When they arrived at their own vehicle, Rider slid

behind the wheel, folding his protection and giving it a shake before he pulled it inside and dropped it into the floorboard behind the passenger seat.

"Should we follow them?" he asked once he had started the car.

"Yes," the older man agreed. "Until this is resolved, you are that girl's guardian, whether she knows it or not."

"Agreed." Rider kicked on the engine and swung the car around. Seeing the taillights of the limo ahead of them, he held back once they had made the turn out onto the actual street and parked a few hundred feet from the gate of their estate so they could monitor them from a discreet distance.

Staring out the glass at the fading light, Thad noted, "At least the rain has stopped."

"Yeah." His son grimaced. "You should call a cab and head back to the hotel. No sense in both of us spending the night crammed in here."

Watching various lights come on throughout the large structure, the older man sighed. "I think we might as well both go. This place looks pretty secure, and there's at least a dozen people inside."

"You think she's safe?" Rider sounded doubtful, picturing her sullen expression beneath her long locks.

"I imagine that she is, at least for now. Let's head back to the hotel, and we'll come back over early before they have a chance to go anywhere, and we can tail them then."

Restarting the engine, Rider reluctantly agreed, "Yeah, I

guess we can't really even be sure that anyone is after her at this point."

Cutting his eyes over to peek at him for a moment, Thad didn't respond. His hands folded in his lap, he turned to stare out the side window instead, keeping what he knew about the Monroes and who might be after them to himself.

TWO

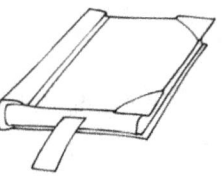

Nostalgic

MERI AWOKE LATER THAN NORMAL. Staring at the room she had lived in all of her life, or at least until she had entered college, she sighed loudly. Little of her personal items remained, and the few that did only made her forlorn.

Sliding from beneath the covers, she slipped on her house shoes and tied her robe around her to cover her thin silk sleeping attire. Taking her time in the bathroom, she brushed her teeth and inspected herself in the mirror, in no hurry to leave the sanctity of her bedroom and private bath. She could hear noises out in the hall and knew that the rest of the house had probably been awake for a while.

A few of her mother's family had come for the funeral, people she had never met, and had left afterwards with little to say to them. Something had happened between her mother and those related to her, and Merideth had learned at an early age it was a subject forever closed. *I'm surprised they came to her funeral,* she admitted to herself, almost glad they had gone home after ignoring her mother's existence her entire life. Whatever happened to cause the rift must have been pretty severe, and the silence between them had been mutual.

It would be her father's nieces, nephews, and cousins causing the noise outside her door—people she felt familiar with and who visited them fairly often. However, losing her mother had ripped her heart from her chest, tearing deep chasms of regret within her, and she did not feel in the mood to welcome visitors, to say the least.

Dropping her robe and gown, Merideth stepped into the shower and washed her soft brown waves along with the rest of her slender frame. Using the dryer to comb it out straight, she applied makeup and then stared at her reflection for a long moment. Deciding it would have to do, she removed a black, light-weight sweater and a pair of slacks from her suitcase.

Finally, she donned her favorite Stuart Weitzman spike-heeled black leather boots. Caressing the studs along the top for a moment, she recalled having purchased them the previous Christmas on a shopping spree with her mother. Her life had changed in the blink of an eye, and she had only begun to realize how deeply her mother's loss would affect her.

Dressed and feeling presentable, she made her way out into the hall. At the far end, her uncle busily pulled suitcases out and placed them next to the door, where the butler would gather them and transport them downstairs. Turning her back on the activity, her fingers trailed the banister as she descended into the kitchen.

"Good morning, ma'am," Glenda addressed her formally.

"Good morning." Meri made herself a cup of coffee, cringing at the laughter of children as they ran through the adjacent hall. Fortunately, they would be leaving soon, and the house would return to its sophisticated calm. *Even I didn't run through the halls screeching,* she lamented as she lifted the warm brew to her lips, her features twisted in a sour grimace.

"Good morning, darling," her father interrupted her thoughts. "Are you going with me to gather your mother's things?"

"Yes." She nodded, a faint pout lingering on her lips.

"Good. I'll see the cousins off, and we'll go as soon as you are ready." He nodded firmly.

Accepting a plate of eggs, bacon, and toast, Merideth sat in the dining room to eat. She had grown up alone in that house and had quickly learned proper manners and behavior befitting the daughter of a wealthy aristocrat. Her father the head of a large corporation, he had moved to the private sector once she had gone to college. Prior to that, he had worked in politics and had spent weeks at a time in D.C., leaving her and her mother to spend their days as they pleased, and a life of luxury pleased her mother very well.

By the time she had finished her meal, the children had

been herded out, and silence surrounded her. Leaning back in her chair, she waited for her father to announce that everyone had departed. When he entered the room to fetch her, his features appeared drawn.

"What's the matter?" she demanded, half afraid to ask.

"Nothing serious," he replied. "One of your uncles voiced concern over your mother's family, but it's nothing you should worry about."

Rising, Meri left the dishes for Glenda to deal with and moved to retrieve her jacket from the hall. "I think we're in for a hard winter," she observed as she smoothed her collar and joined him at the door.

Exiting together, they climbed into her father's slate-colored BMW sedan. "With your mother gone, it most certainly will be," he lamented quietly.

The Monroes weren't big on emotional displays, and she had yet to see her father's grief. Her mother's accident had been a shock, and she felt certain that he was still in some stage of denial. Staring out the window at the winding street, she sighed noisily as they pulled up in front of the church where her mother volunteered.

Exiting the vehicle, the pair made their way inside, where Garrett addressed the receptionist with a familiar tone. "Hello, Madeline."

"Gary," she replied, smiling before her lips scrunched into a tight ring, causing her chin to dimple as she held back her tears. "It was good of you to come," she managed. Picking up a couple of boxes that had been hidden behind her desk, she presented them to the slender girl standing next to him. "For your mother's things," she managed weakly.

Taking the cartons, Meri nodded. "Do you have her key?"

"Here." Her father handed her the small ring. "I'll join you in a moment."

Leaving the pair to discuss business she held no interest in, Merideth made her way down the hall to the wide wooden door. Inserting the key, she allowed the portal to swing wide and stepped inside, dropping the boxes in front of her. Flipping on the switch, the florescent bulbs above her sprang to life, illuminating her mother's desk.

"What in God's name!" she exclaimed, stepping back quickly and calling behind her, "Madeline! Who's been in here?"

Exchanging a glance with Mr. Monroe, the receptionist scurried through the opening between the counter and wall and followed him towards his panic-stricken daughter. "No one," she stated confidently, moving past her and freezing at the sight of the piles of papers, books, and decorations strewn about the small space. Her mouth falling open, she gasped. "How did this happen?"

"Don't touch anything," Garrett warned, reaching out to grasp the arm of the woman in front of him. Pulling gently, he guided her out into the hall. "Go and call the police right now." His upper lip twitched, his emotions getting the better of him for a moment.

Alone with him, Meri squeezed her mother's small keychain in her hand, recalling coming to that very place many times as a child. Her mother had volunteered to head the small food pantry that the church ran when she had been a toddler, and for over twenty years, it had been the only job Ezamay Monroe had ever had.

Staring through the opening at the mess of strewn belongings, Merideth felt anything but nostalgic. "Who did this, Daddy?" she whimpered with a dimpled chin, reaching for his shoulder to lean on.

"I don't know, baby." He wrapped her protectively, hesitating for only a brief moment before confessing, "I'm afraid I haven't been completely honest with you."

Leaning back and cutting her steely blue eyes up at him, she scowled. "What is that supposed to mean?"

"It means that a detective paid me a visit at the office before you arrived to help with the funeral arrangements." He appeared more distraught than she could have imagined. "He seemed convinced that your mother's accident had been intentional, but I had dismissed the idea." Indicating the mess, he sighed. "Perhaps we should have a deeper look."

Stepping back, Meri squealed, "You call him this instant! If this means Mother was a victim of some foul play, you get him down here and let him do his job!"

Reaching into his inner pocket on his customary suit jacket, he retrieved his cell phone and placed the call. His eyes dark, he kept his voice low as he spoke to the detective, informing him that his wife's office had been ransacked and perhaps they needed to do a bit of investigating after all.

FOLLOWING the hostess through the sea of tables a few hours later, Meri hardly noticed the fine white tablecloths of her favorite local restaurant. A large old Victorian-style structure housed the establishment, and she loved the exquisite décor. Tonight, however, she found no comfort amidst it's painted walls and bright white columns that reminded her of strength and stability.

Merideth's world was crumbling around her. Hours ago, she had thought her mother had died as the result of an accident, a stranger who had lost control of his car. Rider stood and pulled out a chair for her, which she accepted with a sour expression, her thoughts trapped on her recent discovery; her mother had been murdered. Her father took the seat directly across from her, and Mr. Bradshaw sat between them on either side of the square table.

Staring at the glass of water the waitress placed before her, she heard her father order a steak, medium rare, for her. Once the meal had been arranged, the men began to speak in low voices, and a look of horror crinkled her features as she demanded, "Daddy, what are you doing?"

His jaw locked angrily for a moment, he recovered, "Whatever do you mean?"

"Why are you discussing this with them? This is a

private matter, not something you should be sharing with strangers!" She glared at the two men who shared their evening.

"My dear, we are hardly strangers," Thaddeus informed her coolly, folding his hands on the table before him. "I am your mother's oldest and dearest friend," he continued, cutting his gaze over at his son as he spoke to silence him.

Unaffected by the glare, Rider chortled. "Honestly, Merideth, I have wondered the same thing. I had never heard of your mother, you, or anyone in your family until my father announced we were coming to her funeral."

Squinting at the younger man's betrayal, Thad continued, "Nonetheless, we are here to protect certain interests that she held."

"Thaddeus, please," Garrett cut in. "Perhaps this is a conversation better suited for a more private location."

"This location will suffice just fine." His voice grew strained as he replied, "Ezamay and I grew up together. We knew each other well. If someone has ended her life prematurely, it falls to me to protect that which she held most dear." His eyes bore into Meri's. "Until further notice, my son will accompany you about your normal routine," he announced.

"What?" she gasped. "And why would that be necessary?"

"Honey, let's not make a scene." Garrett looked around anxiously, then spoke quietly to the man seated to his left.

"Thad, I appreciate the offer. Are you certain that she needs protection? I have security that could handle it, you know."

"Indeed, she is in grave danger," the older man replied, "and I would not trust this matter to anyone else. Rider will watch over her until this situation has been resolved." His tone forceful, he left no room for argument against his decision.

Glancing at the younger man next to her, Meri sighed loudly, then leaned back so her plate could be placed before her. The conversation effectively ended by the arrival of the meal, she watched her father warily as she ate. A strong man, accustomed to being in charge, she wondered at the situation where he would take orders from a stranger, especially one who obviously assumed that he would.

THREE

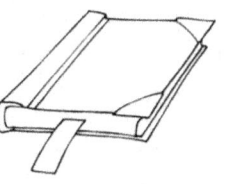

Intuition

MERIDETH STOOD AT THE WINDOW, watching the trio of men outside. Rider lifted a bag and placed it in the trunk of her car, his ponytail floating as he swung his head to look at Thaddeus and laugh. She couldn't hear what they were saying, but the smile on her father's face caused her blood to boil, her intuition going crazy at the situation she found herself in.

"How can they possibly be telling jokes at a time like this?" she seethed aloud to the empty room. Her argument against Rider going to New York with her had been short lived, and she suspected at some point, she would deeply regret not putting up a bigger fight.

But at the moment, how could she? Her father might be practiced at holding a straight face and a stiff upper lip, as he called it, but she knew he had been devastated by her mother's death. The fact that it had been as the result of foul play had only added to the anguish.

Meri was the only thing he had left, and she didn't dare add to his remorse by refusing Rider's protection. However, that didn't mean that she had to like it. Sighing loudly, she picked up her own suitcase that sat next to her feet and carried it to the door. As soon as she exited the structure, her father turned and claimed the bag.

"Meri, you should have asked me to carry that for you," he gently rebuked.

"Why?" she demanded evenly. "I'm not helpless."

Grinning, Rider accepted the small piece of luggage and placed it in the trunk next to his own. "Don't worry, Mr. Monroe. I'm going to take good care of her."

"I'm sure you are." Garrett offered his hand. "Be sure to check in every day or so, and we will keep you informed as to what we have discovered about the assailants."

"Agreed." Rider shook his appendage firmly. Turning to his father, he chuckled. "I'm still not sure I'm the right man for this."

"You're perfect." Thad clapped him on the shoulder. "Just keep her within sight at all times and you'll be fine."

"Hey," Meri snapped. "I resent that you think I need a babysitter, especially one that can't leave at least some time for myself!"

Grinning, Thad winked at her new bodyguard. "He knows what I mean."

Flicking her eyes between them in disgust, she spun

on her heel and climbed behind the wheel. Slamming the door firmly, she started the engine with the intent of leaving her escort behind if he didn't get his rear in the car.

Joining her, Rider shoved his backpack into the floorboard at his feet and closed his own door with a thud. "How long is the drive to your place?" he inquired.

"Five or six hours, depending on the traffic," she replied stiffly, suddenly wishing she had flown. Being stuck in the cramped cabin of her Mercedes with him for that long did not appeal to her in the least. "I usually come down through Highway eighty-one and avoid D.C. and New Jersey entirely."

"All right," he agreed, pulling a book out of the backpack, "but if we take the Jersey route, I can show you a bit of the area where I grew up."

"This isn't a holiday," she informed him curtly, adjusting her grip on the wheel. "Read your book and let me handle the driving."

Snorting loudly, Rider cracked the pages to locate his place without further argument. She had been short with him every time she spoke, and she hoped at some point he would get the hint that they weren't going to be friends— not if she could help it. *The sooner he figures that out, the sooner I get my life back,* she rationalized.

Following her normal path, Meri put them on the highway cleanly, and they had ridden for over an hour before Rider stopped turning pages. Having turned in the seat so that he no longer sat square to the back, he leaned against the door and watched her covertly.

Her long straight locks hanging a good six inches past her shoulders, it parted on the left side and formed a swoop as it hung down and tucked behind her right ear. He liked the cute little point of her nose and the soft curve of her chin, especially as she ground her teeth while her thoughts turned.

"Why didn't we fly?" he eventually dared to ask.

Her lips forming a thin line for a moment, she scowled and then replied, "I hate flying and always have. Daddy has a private jet that he bought when I was a little girl, but it didn't help."

"You're afraid of planes? That's a pretty irrational fear." He chuckled, staring at the ear that she exposed by re-tucking the hairs behind it.

"I fly when I have to," she bit angrily, "but I moved to New York so I could have my career and still be close enough to drive home when I wanted to visit. Anything else you want to know?"

Rider could feel the animosity rolling off of her stiff form. "I don't know anything about you," he kept his reply low, not rising to her challenge. "If I'm going to look out for you, it would be better if I did."

"Let's start with you," she countered evenly. "Why does Thaddeus think I need *you* to look after me? My father pays his security a pretty penny, and they are all highly qualified."

"I don't know." Rider blinked at her statement of the obvious. "Maybe he thinks I will take the job more seriously, considering our relationship."

"What relationship?" Her tone grew tense. "Why don't you get to the point! You and your father turn up after my mother's been"—she hesitated, drawing a ragged breath before her voice fell to a loud whisper—"my mother's been murdered." She sniffed.

Daring to touch her, his hand squeezed her shoulder as he soothed, "Hey, don't get so upset. I'm not the enemy here. Dad and I only want to help."

She stiffened at his choice of words, considering the man next to her. "Who are you then? And why does Thad think that he is my mother's 'oldest and dearest friend,' as he put it."

Rolling his tongue for a moment, Rider considered his response before he admitted, "I don't really know. I knew nothing about you or her until my father called to get me on the plane."

"I thought you lived in New Jersey," she spat, wiping at an escaped tear.

"No, not since I graduated from high school," he confessed. "I joined the army and left, then moved to New Orleans after my tour was over."

"New Orleans…" Meri imagined the town she had seen only in pictures. "That's a long way from home."

"Yes," he agreed, squaring himself in his seat. "Hurricane Katrina pretty much destroyed it while I was in the service, so when I got out, I went down to make myself useful and help with the reconstruction."

"Wasn't that like ten years ago?" she demanded, not trusting his explanation.

"Yeah, it was," he agreed, "but the city grew on me, and I stayed. I used my GI bill at LSU, there in Baton Rouge."

Realizing he had sounded like an educated man and that his story appeared plausible, Meri sighed. Her head hurt from the emotional rollercoaster she had been on, and thinking about whether or not he had lied to her didn't help. "Fine," she muttered. "You live in Louisiana, you were in the Army, and you are going to keep my mother's killer from doing the same to me," she simplified.

"Yeah," he agreed with a firm nod. "That sums it up. So, what do I need to know about you?"

"I'm a private person," she snapped. "That's what you need to know about me. I grew up in that house with my parents, went to design school at UCLA, and I work for a firm in New York. I'm married to my career, hate entanglements, and have no plans to ever get involved with a man or a family."

"Huh." He grinned, watching her profile as she described the essence of her being in one brief paragraph. "Design school," he repeated the seemingly safest portion.

"Yes." She smiled slightly. "I'm an interior decorator, and I have a very promising future. I work for a major firm and am on the fast track to owning my own one day."

"I see." He nodded. "Well, hopefully we won't have any problems that delay any of that for you."

"What's that supposed to mean?" she quipped.

"It means, between our dads and the police, hopefully they will find the man or men behind your mother's accident quickly and your fast track won't suffer any traffic jams." He chuckled as he turned to look out his window, ending their conversation as abruptly as he had started it.

FOUR

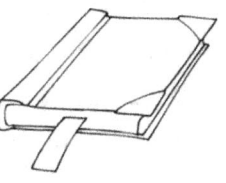

Danger Zone
_____

RIDER STARED OUT THE WINDOW, watching the brightly colored trees zooming past. He had missed fall in the north for the past few years and looked at this latest adventure as an excuse to enjoy this one. Besides, the moody female next to him could prove to be a handful, and he needed to evaluate his take on the situation before they went any further.

No entanglements, she said. Does bumping uglies count? he wondered. He had been scoping her out at the funeral, but under her coat, there hadn't been much to see. Last night at dinner, he had gotten a better look, and this morning, she had set his groin on fire. *Damn, she's hot,* he admitted to himself.

Rider had always liked tall, slender types. He wasn't into big tits or round butts and really liked a woman who took care of herself. Not daring to look over at her, he had already memorized the thin thighs and muscled biceps that were outlined by her snuggly-fitted sweater. *Yeah, she'd do for a few days or weeks of happy time.*

Beyond that, he wasn't really looking for a permanent relationship any more than she was and had always thought of long term commitment as the danger zone—that place where life became a grind, sucking the joy out of pretty much everything. He had discovered this after spending almost two years with the same girl and had vowed to himself that it would never happen again.

Massaging his lower lip while he chewed on it, he squirmed in his seat. They had been on the road for a couple of hours, and his bladder had been protesting more loudly with each passing mile. "Any chance at a pit stop?" he finally asked.

Meri indicated a few tall signs in the distance. "Sure. I'll take the next exit, and we can stop at one of those."

Straightening as they pulled into a parking space, he climbed out of the leather-covered seat. "That's a nice ride, by the way," he complimented, hanging back and allowing her to walk through the double glass doors before him. Watching her rear end twitch as she glided along, he wore a lopsided grin, imagining removing the garment covering it before she disappeared into the ladies' room.

Relieving himself in the men's facilities, he washed up and went in search of coffee. "You want some of this?" he offered when she joined him. Each taking a cup, they paid for a tank of gas at the pump and returned to the interstate, heading north once more.

Setting back comfortably, he inquired, "Any idea who might want to kill your mother? Or why?"

Inhaling a short sniff, Merideth winced. "No." The question had been like a slap in the face, a cold reminder of her loss.

"Ah, sorry." He adjusted his legs anxiously and took a sip from his cup. "I know it's not pleasant to talk about. It's just that we need to figure out where the danger might be coming from, if you know what I mean."

"I don't think there's any danger," she replied crisply, "at least not to me. My mother and I had almost nothing in common and lived very different lives."

"Ok, then who would have wanted to hurt her do you think?"

"I can't imagine that anyone would." She leaned against her hand and propped her head up by placing her elbow on the window. "But obviously, that idea is mistaken. Someone ransacked her office, perhaps searching for something. Maybe it wasn't her that they wanted but something she had come to possess." Meri had often wondered about the woman who spent so much of her time working with those who were less fortunate, and briefly considered that one of them might have taken advantage of her good nature.

Nodding, the idea seemed plausible. "Well, in that case, the question would be if they found it," he agreed.

"Yes, but we really have no way of knowing. We have no idea what they were looking for, either." She sighed, weary with thinking about it.

Allowing her to retreat into her silence, Rider continued to consider the situation. He had been surprised by his father's call but had obediently gotten on the next flight to Washington to meet up with him. Upon his arrival, Thad had filled him in on what he knew, which was simply that a woman from his past had died suddenly, and he suspected foul play.

His mind turning, he went over the conversations they had held, where his father had described Ezamay Monroe as a dear friend. He briefly considered that the two of them might have been lovers before recalling that she was actually the same age as his own mother and therefore only eighteen years old when he was born. *Dad would have been quite a stud to land two young things like them back then.*

A darker thought crowded his mind, realizing that they could have been involved after he was born, and his father had therefore had an affair with her. "How old are you?" he demanded gruffly, disturbed by the idea.

"Twenty-four." Meri sighed, still sitting in her slouched position.

Doing some quick math, he worked out that her mother had been twenty-six when the girl was born.

"How long have your mother and father been married?" he pushed.

"What's that got to do with anything?" she bit angrily. "Are you implying that I'm illegitimate?"

"No." He chopped the air with a stiff hand. "I'm trying to draw all the connections. My father claims to have had a relationship with your mother when she was young—a child in fact. He said they were neighbors when he was a kid. I'm just trying to figure out when your old man came into the picture. He's rich, isn't he? Some kind of politician?"

Shifting to glare at him, Meri felt her stomach turn at the idea that her father could somehow be connected with her mother's death.

He had behaved strangely, not telling her there were questions about Ezamay's accident until he had been forced to by the disheveled office.

"I don't like what you're insinuating," she informed him, cutting him a quick glance as sharp as any knife.

"I'm not insinuating anything," he replied matter-of-factly. "I'm merely pulling out all the evidence and examining it before I make any judgements."

Her eyes narrowed at the road, she gripped the wheel firmly, her knuckles turning white as the blood was forced out of them.

"I'm twenty-four. I was born the year after my parents were married. She met my father while working on his campaign for the senate. They dated and fell in love, and that, as they say, is that."

"Did your mother ever mention my father or any other Bradshaws?"

"No. She didn't talk about her life before she married my father." She blinked back tears. "I think her family was poor when she was growing up, and that's why she spent all that time working at the food bank. Like she was making up for something in her past. I have no idea what they are like, as I had never met any of them before she died."

"Never?" He sounded skeptical.

"Never," she resounded forcefully.

Clenching his jaw, Rider mentally measured the possibility. *And if she felt guilty about her relationship with Dad, she definitely would have kept it a secret as well,* he surmised.

Turning back to his window, he allowed the new information to stew until they arrived at a high-rise building and turned into the parking area below it.

"How much does it cost you to park here every month?" he asked, recalling that cars and New York weren't made for one another.

"It's part of my lease." She shrugged. "I have a good education and a great job. I don't have to worry about the expense of my car."

Climbing out, she retrieved her bag and waited for him to claim his. Her heels clicking on the asphalt, she led him across to the elevators inside the small chamber and pushed the button to her floor.

A few minutes later, she unlocked her apartment and allowed the door to swing wide as she entered. "Make yourself at home," she offered out of polite habit and her tone anything but inviting.

"Thanks." He grimaced, growing weary of her ingratitude. "Do I have a room, or is this it?" He indicated the sofa before him with an outstretched palm. Glancing around the room, he scowled. *For an interior designer, this place sure is a mess.*

Her drafting table to his left and straight in front of the door, it lay beneath a thick layer of rolled-up papers and material swatches. "I guess you haven't gotten around to doing your own place?" he prodded, indicating the pile of work.

"No," she called over her shoulder as she sauntered down the hall. "You can sleep in here." She smacked the door frame to the spare bedroom lightly as she passed by. Reaching the end of the hall, she entered her own quarters and closed the door behind her.

Continuing his inspection, his eyes followed the left-hand wall from the workspace to the far-left corner, which had been set up as a dining area, complete with a folding table and only three chairs, all adorned with a few pieces of cloth in various shades tossed across them. The kitchen sat off to the right, also against the exterior wall, and a small bar covered in tiny furniture pieces like you would put in a doll house separated it from the living area where he stood.

Also covered in material samples, the half-hidden sofa before him faced the right-hand wall, where a large floor-to-ceiling bookcase stood, dotted with mismatched decorations and a few shelves of texts.

Kneeling down to have a closer look at the bottom row, a trio of leather-bound books had garnered his attention, and he lifted one to peek inside.

"That was my mother's," Meri informed him curtly.

He hesitated, surprised she had snuck up on him in stocking feet. "We had a few books like this at home when I was growing up—with old musty pages that smelled funny."

"Well, that one is a family heirloom. Would you mind putting it back and not touching things that don't belong to you?" she snapped, moving past him and into the kitchen to prepare their dinner.

Hearing the catch in her voice, Rider complied.

Placing the heavy tome next to the others, he noted that the spines were all blank, leaving it to the imagination what could be inside.

His finger tracing the binding, he felt an odd tingle in his gut, and the memory of his father's similar taste in reading material percolated in the back of his mind. Standing, he formulated a plan, fully intending to have a closer look at the rare volumes after she had gone to bed.

FIVE

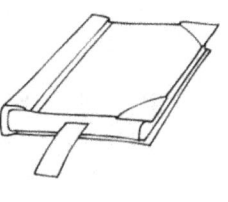

Nothing New

"I'M GOING WITH YOU," Rider insisted loudly, stretching to tower over her in a more demanding manner.

"No." She shook her head as she placed a few of the items from her laden drafting table into a soft-sided brief-case. "I told you there isn't any reason for the people who hurt my mother to be after me. Besides, the clients I am visiting today are rather fragile. They wouldn't take kindly to your tagging along."

"Yeah, right." He scoffed. "I'm coming even if I have to leap into a cab and yell *follow that car* to the driver to get there." The change in his voice when he tossed out the cliché gave him a brief chuckle before he managed to deepen his frown. "Seriously, Meri. I can't look after you—not the way you need to be. You don't know enough to say for sure that you aren't a target."

Ignoring the pleading tone of his voice, she closed her

bag and slung her purse over her shoulder. Running her hands over her fine linen suit, she huffed angrily before dropping her shades over her eyes. "Do whatever you feel you have to do," she challenged before closing the door behind her.

Hoisting his own backpack and getting himself together, he flew out the door and didn't wait for the elevator. Dashing down the stairs, he hoped he could clear the six flights before she could make it to her car parked in the garage.

Racing through the lobby, he dodged a few people and paused on the sidewalk. Spying a taxi, he trotted over and opened the door. Climbing into the back seat, he watched the mouth of the tunnel at the far end of the walk.

"Where to, buddy?" the driver demanded when he didn't speak.

"Give me a minute," he breathed before slapping the seat in front of him. "There!" He pointed at the dark Mercedes. "Follow that black car, and don't you dare lose her!"

"Are you kidding me?" The man twisted in an attempt to glare at him.

"No, I'm not," Rider's voice grew strained. "Trust me. There's a hefty tip in it for you if you get me to her destination without her knowing."

Shaking his head, the cabbie pulled out into traffic, maintaining a safe distance as they traveled.

A short time later, they had cleared the bulk of the traffic and were headed out towards Williamsburg. "That your girl-friend?" he demanded when she pulled into a parking area attached to a high-rise tower of condos.

"No," Rider snapped, tossing a fifty and a couple of twenties at him. "Keep the change," he muttered as he climbed out and moved quickly to keep her in his sights when she entered the glass-covered structure.

Inside, he watched her go in an elevator, cursing under his breath as she obviously had no clue that she had been followed, nor was she paying any attention to the people and area around her.

Standing in front of the metal doors, he waited until the car stopped on the twenty-second floor.

When it began to descend after a brief pause, he felt safe in assuming that she had gotten off at that level and punched the button for himself. Adjusting his pack over his shoulder, he felt relieved that he had thought to bring the bag of supplies that would help him blend in with the surroundings more easily, as a good degree of stealth would be required if he wanted to keep his presence unknown.

Arriving on the correct floor a few minutes later, he cautiously stepped off the lift to have a look around. The area looking like a long, slender waiting area, a few modern-décor chairs and tables dotted the hallway, providing places to sit between the doors. Choosing one at the end, where a glass wall afforded him a spectacular view of the city, he pulled out his sketchbook and began a new page.

Thinking he would capture the incredible skyline, he glanced up the hall regularly, hoping he wouldn't be noticed when she exited the apartment she had entered before his arrival.

Working quickly on a blank page, he filled it with a rough outline and began darkening in the details.

His mind stuck on the girl, his efforts slowed. Glaring up the passage, he thought about their morning before she had left the apartment without him.

The night before, after Meri had been in her room with the light off for quite a while, he had ventured into the living area to collect one of the books she had been so possessive of. Taking it back to his sparsely furnished quarters, he had flipped through pages, noting that it had changed hands and authors a few times over the years.

Jolted awake by her movement in the kitchen the next morning, he discovered he had not returned the diary to the shelf. He had felt grateful he had been thinking ahead and closed the door while he snooped, but with her presence, he would have to hide it in his room and hope she didn't notice it had been taken until he could safely put it back.

Staring at his drawing while their argument played through his mind, he scowled. Flipping the page to a fresh one, he traced the outline of something else, trying to distract himself from his dark thoughts.

Hearing the elevator chime at the far end of the hall, he watched as a man in shorts and a Hawaiian shirt stepped off of it.

His hat turned backwards and shiny, reflective shades covering his eyes, the stubble beneath them darkened his face and gave him a disheveled appearance. In his hand, he carried a large canvas bag with a few long rolls of paper or cloth sticking out the top.

Rider's heart skipped a beat at the idea that anything could be hidden inside such canisters, and he envisioned hunting rifles and swords as he swallowed nervously. Closing his sketchbook slowly, he debated his next move, when the man in question knocked firmly on one of the doors. The portal opened, and a shrill voice carried quickly through the air.

Dropping his drawing materials, Rider was on the stranger in no time, knocking his parcels out of his hands and flinging him face first against the wall across from the entrance. Holding him firmly by a twisted appendage behind his back, he demanded, "What are you doing here?"

"Rider, stop it!" Merideth squealed, closing the door and joining them in the hall.

Glancing over to see she hadn't been harmed, he growled, "You know this guy?"

"Yes, I know him." Her hands flew to her hips in obvious disgust. "He's a runner for my office, and I was just giving him a lecture about his being out of uniform!"

Considering the explanation, Rider released his grip, allowing the young man to have his arm back. "Oh," he finally managed, smoothing back his hair and adjusting his ponytail. "Sorry. I thought you might be in danger."

Scowling at him, Meri didn't budge. "I told you to stay away from me." She kept her voice low. "I don't need a bodyguard."

Gathering his scattered samples, the newcomer placed them in his bags and handed them to her. "I'm sorry about the clothes, Miss Monroe," he said sheepishly. "I swear that it won't happen again," he groveled, licking his lips anxiously.

"See that it doesn't." She snatched the sacks away. Still giving Rider the evil eye, the pair waited until he had gone before she exploded. "These are very important clients!"

"Yeah, I got that." He shifted anxiously, then pointed at his gear by the far window. "Look, I don't need to come inside. I'll be down there when you're done, so go take care of your customers, and then we'll go get something to eat."

Grinding her teeth, Meri watched him trudge back to his seat and pick up the drawing materials. The idea of a man trying to impose his will upon her was nothing new, and she vowed she wouldn't let him get the better of her. Adjusting her load, she forced the frown off of her face and slipped back inside, hoping she could make it through the rest of the appointment unscathed.

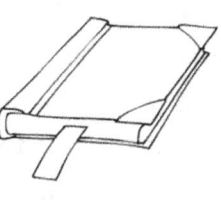

SIX

In Charge

STORMING through the door of her apartment, Meri gave it a heavy slam, leaving Rider in the hall outside. Not hesitating, he wrenched open the portal and stomped inside. "That was uncalled for!"

"Uncalled for," she mimicked. "This whole situation is uncalled for! You had no right following me today." She held her palms up, indicating him with a flattened hand angrily. "I told you you would only be in the way. You could have gotten me in trouble. You could have gotten me fired!"

"I would not." He pulled off his jacket and dropped it over the couch.

"That doesn't go there," she growled through clenched teeth and pointed at the coatrack next to her desk.

"Oh, sorry," he mocked her. "I can see what a neat freak you are!" he taunted sarcastically.

"Hey, it's unfinished. That doesn't mean that it isn't clean!" she countered angrily. "You know, I've had about enough of you! Your being here is pointless," she screeched, noticing at that moment that things were beyond their normal level of chaos in her home. "What did you do?" she demanded, indicating the pile of books in front of the sofa.

Staring at her drafting table and the contents that had been shoved onto the floor, he caught her arm and pulled her behind him, closer to the door. His attention on the hall, he could see that all the lights had been left on, and pillows lay in his doorway. "Shit!"

"Oh my God. What happened?" she asked shakily, realizing there had been a break-in while they had been away for the day.

"Someone's been here," he simplified. "We should go outside and call the police in case they're still here."

"Bull shit," she screamed, pushing past him and stomping down the hall. Glancing into her former roommate's bedroom, she pulled her phone out of her pocket and dialed while moving to her own. "Hey! Did you come and get your stuff today?" she bit angrily.

Anxiously following behind, Rider wondered if there was an ex involved that needed to be considered as a suspect. Stopping at his doorway, he scowled at the mess that had been made, with the bed stripped and items pulled out of the closet. Waiting until she ended the call, he surveyed her bedroom as well, but as soon as she hung up, he demanded, "We need to get outside and call the cops. Don't touch anything!"

"Why? So they can dust for prints?" She scoffed. "They didn't find anything at my mother's office, so I doubt we would have any luck here."

"Did your boyfriend do this?" He indicated the collection of items she had begun to paw through in the living room.

"I don't have, nor did I have, a boyfriend. I had a roommate who moved here with me from UCLA. She denies it." Meri's voice changed as she poked around the contents of the bookcases. Lifting a few pieces, she stated, "My mother's books are gone."

"What!" Rider dropped down to help her search, but the large leather-bound tomes would be hard to miss. "Shit," he repeated. Realizing one of them hadn't been there to be taken, he got to his feet and went into his bedroom. Kneeling down in front of the tall chest of drawers, he ran a hand underneath and felt elated to discover the outline of the text when he made contact but couldn't get a hold on it.

"Meri, I need you!" he called. Standing to lean the wooden tower over, he indicated his secret. "Grab that, would ya?"

Lifting her mother's treasure, she exploded, "Why was my mother's book under your dresser, and how did you know it was there?"

"Later. Right now, we need to get the hell out of here."

He shoved her towards the door. "Pack a bag and make sure you have everything you'll need for a few days, including your phone, charger, and clothes, but one suitcase only."

"Wait just a God damned minute!" she bellowed back. "Who put you in charge?"

Seizing her by her upper arms, he lifted her slightly so that her feet partially lost contact with the floor. "Merideth Monroe, I'm not a violent man, and I would never hit a woman. But if you don't do as I say right the fuck now, I'm going to give you the spanking you never had, and you aren't going to enjoy it!"

Her eyes wide, her mouth formed a wide *oh* before he released her. Staggering back a few steps, she pressed her right hand flat against her chest above her perky bosom. "Well, I never!" she breathed.

"Nope. Neither have I, but there's a first time for everything." He spun around, locating his suitcase amongst the scattered articles and checking the contents. When he glanced up, she still stood in the door, petrified by fear. "Move!" he screamed.

Turning and dodging into her own room, she grabbed the bag she had taken to her parents' place for her mother's funeral. Flopping it on the bed and throwing it open, she pulled out the bag of dirty clothes and tossed it aside and then filled the case with fresh panties, bras, and blouses. Taking two pairs of dress slacks, she also included two pairs of shorts, a pair of jeans, and canvas tennis shoes.

Moving to the bathroom, she retrieved her toothbrush

and shoved it into her makeup bag. Snatching the brush off the counter, she decided there wouldn't be room for her hair dryer and went with what she had. Zipping it with a small bit of effort, she hoisted it off the bed and turned to find him glaring at her. "What? I'm going," she lamented.

"I know," he breathed more calmly, reaching to take the suitcase from her. His backpack over his shoulder and his bag in the other hand, he instructed, "Lead the way, and if anyone jumps us, you run. You don't stop and you don't look back. Out the exit and down the street."

"Down the street?" She frowned inside the elevator. "Aren't we taking my car?"

"No." He shook his head, his ponytail hopping across his back. "It would be too easy to spot us. First we get out of town, and then we pick up a low-profile vehicle." The doors parted and the couple stepped out into the lobby. At the exit, they turned and moved down the walk in unison. "Get in that cab," he commanded, indicating the yellow taxi with his left fist that still clutched the handle to her bag.

Doing as she was told, Meri slid across the seat, and he shoved the suitcases and his backpack in after her. Able to close the door, he demanded, "How far can you take us?"

Giving him a sharp glare, Merideth interrupted. "JFK International, please."

Rider relaxed into his seat, meeting her gaze. He could see by the tightness of her jaw that she had a plan, and whatever it was would work as far as getting them away from her home. *Besides, the airport is a good choice,* he mentally praised. From there, they could leave in any number of directions, and if anyone was after them, they would have a harder time picking up their trail.

Arriving at one of the terminals almost an hour later, he scowled when she used her credit card to pay for the trip. After the yellow vehicle pulled away, he stated calmly, "I think we need some cash. I don't like plastic—in case anyone is able to use it to track us."

"And who do you think is after us? This isn't a spy movie. Ordinary people can't track someone through their credit cards," she sneered. Seeing that he watched around them anxiously, she sighed. "Ok, Mr. Bond, let's go get a car and figure out what we should do next."

Moving through the sliding glass doors, they made their way over to a counter and were greeted by a slender blonde. Asking the sales attendant for specifics, Rider decided on the most ordinary sounding vehicle and declared, "Yup. We'll take that one."

Climbing into a navy-blue Toyota Camry a short time later, he cast a quick glance over his shoulder at their bags in the back seat.

From the passenger side, Meri scowled. "You should have let me drive. I know my way around here better than you."

"It doesn't matter," he countered evenly. "You're going to give me directions for the shortest route out of here and keep an eye out around us for anyone who seems to be following us."

"Aye, aye, captain," she continued to mock him, earning a dark glance before she pointed out a turn that would take them west and then north. Sulking as they rode, she stared out the window in disgust while the sun set and the bright lights of the city came on around them.

SEVEN

Bloodlines
_____

MERI HAD FALLEN asleep with her head pressed against the window and found herself jolted awake when he shook her firmly. "What?" she stammered, looking around, disoriented before she recalled her trashed apartment and their bid to escape. "Where are we?" she tacked on quietly.

"Camden," he replied softly, getting their bags out of the car. "I drove around and made lots of turns and course changes until I was certain we weren't being tailed."

"And why are we here?" She stretched, too exhausted to sound annoyed at the moment.

"This is where I grew up." He tossed his backpack over his shoulder and indicated the room he had secured for them. "We moved away when I was about ten. It just felt right...coming here."

Looking up and down the walk, she could see the row of plain doors facing her, with the large blue and orange sign glowing on the corner of the lot. "You brought me to a cheap motel?" she growled, finding her strength and her aggravation showing.

"Yeah." He grinned slightly and shoved open the door. "Get inside."

Wearing a heavy pout, she stomped past him, noting that the floor appeared linoleum, only in a wood pattern. "Great. There isn't even carpet." Glaring at the pair of beds, that would be the only good news if she could call it that; he didn't expect her to share. "I want my own room," she informed him.

"Fat chance." He dropped her suitcase on the mattress closest to the bathroom and vanity area. "We're in trouble, and that means the best thing we can do is to stay away from familiar things and places where someone might expect to find us. You being a *sophisticated* little rich girl, I doubt anyone would think to look for you at Motel 6."

His twist on the word *sophisticated* gave her stomach a jolt. He hadn't spoken civilly to her since they had arrived at her place the night before, or had it been two days ago since they drove home from Virginia? Tired, she couldn't remember and gave up with a sigh. "Fine. I don't understand why we didn't go back to my father's house if you were worried about someone coming after us. That place is a fortress."

"Yeah, and that's the first place they would look for you." He opened his backpack and pulled out her mother's book. "I wish I had hidden them all...now that the other two are gone. We have no way of knowing if this one is what they were after or not."

"Give me that," she snapped, reaching for the heavy text. Taking it from him and placing it on the small square table, she noted that the flat surface had been bolted to the wall dividing the bedroom and the small bathroom. "This room is awful," she muttered, opening the thick pages and noticing the script.

"This is our family diary," she informed him, her fingers lightly trailing over stanzas that resembled a poem. "I'm supposed to add my story to the back of it," her voice cracked.

"Well, not tonight you're not." He gripped her arm firmly and turned her towards the beds. "I'll wait outside while you get changed."

Her eyes wide, she gasped. "I didn't bring anything to sleep in."

A muscle flexing in his jaw as he ground his teeth together, he inhaled deeply. "Fine. I'll give you a shirt, and you can sleep in that." Pulling one from his bag, he tossed it on top of hers and headed for the door. "And don't get any bright ideas," he cautioned. "This is exactly what I was instructed to do."

"What is?" She raised her trembling chin defiantly.

"If anything happened, I was told by your old man to take you someplace no one would look and to keep you safe." Pausing, he spoke to her over his shoulder. "That's what I'm going to do, Meri. I'm going to keep you safe."

Opening the exit, he stepped outside to give her some privacy while she changed and adjusted to her meager accommodations.

"Poor girl," he muttered, pulling out a pack of cigarettes and opening the cellophane wrap. Her life had been turned upside down, and there was nothing either of them could do about it. Lighting one, he took a long drag, his eyes roaming over the parking lot and adjacent streets anxiously.

Inside the room, Merideth took the shirt and closed herself in the tiny bathroom. Pulling off her fine business suit, she considered that it had probably cost more than the man outside's entire wardrobe. The idea giving her an odd flutter in her chest, she slipped on his shirt, noting that it hung just low enough to pass for a very short skirt.

Gathering her things, she laid them on the counter outside the door to the toilet and looked over the selection of items. A rolled trash bag lay next to the individually wrapped plastic cups and plastic ice bucket. *I think I'm going to be sick,* she thought to herself. *This place is shit!*

Unrolling the spare bag, she opened it and dropped her clothing inside before placing it next to her suitcase. Deciding it needed to be moved, she shifted it over to the only chair in the room. Hearing a knock on the door, announcing the return of her companion, she briefly thought about hiding her bare legs under her sheets but forced herself to move calmly as she pulled back the blankets and adjusted her two pillows.

Locking the privacy latch, Rider watched her covertly,

admiring her smooth skin and the brief shot of panties he received before she hid them beneath her bedding. "We'll stay here for a day or two until we figure things out," he informed her as he hoisted his cotton tee over his head and exposed his bare chest for her.

His six-pack well defined, he had obviously taken care of himself even after leaving the military. Dropping his jeans, he also demonstrated his lack of modesty before strange women. Tossing everything but his grey boxer briefs into a pile behind the door, he stretched out on his own bed and draped the sheet across him. Reaching over with his long arm, he plunged the room into darkness and rolled onto his side, his back to her, and drifted off to sleep.

Meri awoke to the sound of movement in the blackness, and her breath caught in her throat. Daring to turn over, she could see his outline by the dim light filtering in from around the thick drapes.

"I'm sorry. Did I wake you?" his thick voice comforted her.

"It's ok. I'm an early riser." She smiled to herself. "Why aren't you sleeping?"

He shrugged, then reached for the switch to turn on the light above his bed. "I'm anxious, I guess. Nothing has gone right since I left NOLA." He sighed.

"NOLA?" she repeated, sitting up herself and adjusting her blankets across her lap.

"New Orleans, Louisiana." He chuckled. "I guess you could call it a nickname."

"I see," she agreed. "Well, is it too early for breakfast? And I'd really like to have a plan," she informed him, holding her tone even.

"Yeah, you struck me as an appointment-book girl." He chuckled, throwing back his bedding and getting to his feet. Pulling on the jeans he had taken off only a few hours before, he continued. "All right, we'll have a look around today and decide what we should do next. I do want to have a look at that book of yours—see if there's anything special about it. I peeked through it the other night, but none of it really made any sense to me. Maybe it will to you."

Meri watched him pick up his pack of cigarettes and move towards the exit. "I didn't realize you smoked," she informed him bluntly.

"I don't." He reached for the door. "It's just something to do so people don't wonder why I'm hanging around outside while you take care of business," he explained before it clicked shut behind him.

Leaping out of the bed, Merideth stripped off his shirt and her panties and adjusted the water to the shower. Making it quick, she had bathed and redressed in under ten minutes. Opening the door, she smiled at the man leaning against a pole next to their car, his tall frame accentuated by the light that had been growing brighter as the sun rose. Stepping back to allow him to enter, she said meekly, "I want to thank you for looking out for me."

Cutting his eyes over at her, he wondered if she were actually up to something before dismissing the idea, at least for the moment. "There's a pancake house around the corner. We'll head over there when you're ready to eat." Lightly touching the text that had remained open on the table, he admired the script for its neatness. "Who did you say wrote this?"

"The women in my family." She moved closer to him, also admiring the poem. Turning the page, she indicated a name scrawled along the top of the next. "My mother said it has gone from mother to daughter for generations, each of us adding to it."

"I see. So it's a history of your family." He leaned nearer to inspect the words. "Is that a date?" He pointed at the pen marks next to the name.

"Yes, I think that it is." She leaned in closer herself. "It says sixteen-eighty-eight. Can that be right?" she gasped.

"I guess that it is." He smiled. "Don't worry. This book isn't going anywhere, and we'll be able to trace your maternal bloodlines easily enough. After we eat of course." He rubbed his belly for emphasis.

"Sure, we can go eat," she agreed, closing the text. "Hide this in your bag, though. I don't want to leave it out in the open."

Gently shoving it back into his backpack, he worked to get it to slide over his sketchbook, which had caught her eye. Grasping at the bag, she removed the thinner sheaf of pages and flipped it open.

"What's this?" she demanded, surprised that it held drawings of various people and things. Turning the pages slowly, she wondered at the detail of the drawings. Lifting her gaze, she waited for him to explain.

Her mother's book safely inside his pack, he zipped it up and closed his collection of work, removing it from her grasp. "I like to draw," he informed her stiffly, a little self-conscious about the admission.

"They're nice." She grinned up at him.

"Yeah, well." He dropped the pad on the table and indicated the door. "It's just something I like to do," he stated flatly, unwilling to give her any more than that. He had taken enough ribbing over his doodles and wasn't about to open himself up to any from her.

Taking care of their physical needs, the couple relaxed into each other's company and had achieved a small amount of harmony between them by the time they arrived back in their room. Retrieving the book he had carefully hidden while Meri moved her suitcase, Rider took the cushioned, stationary mini-couch in the corner next to the table while she scooted the chair in closer.

"So this is your family history?" he asked in the warmest tone she had heard from him in days.

"Yes. My mother said it had been written by the women who came before us, for a few centuries it would appear." She opened the front cover and ran her fingers over the inside page of names. "Look. It's like an index of us."

"And after you add your part, you'll give it to your daughter," he surmised, his fingers brushing hers as they both caressed the list.

Pulling her hand away quickly as if he had scorched her, she remained silent. Then sitting up straighter, she demanded, "So when you were snooping, you didn't see anything of interest? Why would anyone want a ratty old book?"

"Well, I did see a few things," he confessed, pushing it so that it lay flat on the table more evenly between them. "See? This isn't English." He indicated the first few pages. Turning them, he reached almost the halfway point of the text. "It starts to have a bit of English here." He tapped the page.

Leaning forward, Meri perused the passage, finding that it held a name at the top, as the pages before: *Judith Knight*. The history briefly defined her relationship with one Rufus Lister, including their marriage, children, and life together. She froze when she caught the words *City of Camden*. "Where did you say we are?" She pointed with a trembling digit.

"Yeah, that's where we are, unless there's another one." He looked around them anxiously, a chill falling over him.

"I should have brought my laptop," she lamented. "We could have done a little research."

"I'm sure they have a library," he suggested, his eyes shifting to study her. He had noticed during breakfast that she appeared to have abandoned her makeup, at least for the time being. Her skin a smooth pink, his fingers yearned to find out if it was as soft as it appeared.

"I don't like this." Her blue eyes met his. "If my family

history is here in this town where you grew up…" Her voice trailed away. "Maybe your father was telling the truth. Maybe he did know my mother when she was younger."

"It seems possible." He smiled at her, taken with the urge to kiss her. Leaning slightly towards his target, he exhaled softly, closing his eyes.

Sensing his intent, Merideth shoved her chair back and stood abruptly. "Has it not occurred to you that you and I might be related?" she pointed out bluntly.

The wind knocked out of him, her words fell like a punch in the gut. As a matter of fact, it had, but he wasn't about to admit that out loud. "No way." He chuckled, rising beside her. "If we were, we'd have met before now," he rationalized.

"No, we might not have. My mother never spoke of her life before she met my father. If her family was from here, I never heard of it, and the few family members from her side that I have met kept their distance and didn't say much," she informed him curtly. Flipping the pages, she searched frantically for the final segment. "I need to know what she wrote."

Locating her mother's portion, her eyes followed the lines of text. Her features drawn, she slowly sank back down onto the stiff seat. In her own words, the younger Ezamay described her deep devotion to the one she loved with "the entirety" of her being—a man named Teddy. Her lips moving as she read her mother's words, Meri's heart thumped uncomfortably against the walls of her chest—an outing, where the two of them had visited the river and shared a day making love. Her stomach turned, realizing for the first time in her life that her father had not been her mother's first sexual encounter, as she had been led to believe. "I think I'm going to be sick," she whispered.

His hand sliding up her back, Rider comforted, "It's ok. I'm sure she loved your father," he lied, not sure of anything at the moment.

"Yes, I'm sure she did." She sniffed. *But she loved someone else first.* The words her mother had used to describe the afternoon were so unlike the rigid and composed woman she knew. *This was a girl, carefree and unhindered*—certainly unlike anything Meri would ever use to describe Ezamay Monroe.

"Should we look for a library?" he asked softly, concerned at her obvious agitation.

"No." She bit her quivering lip. "I don't want to know any more." She turned the page and slid her fingers over the top of a poem, not written in English. She had been unaware that her mother spoke more than one language, and the discovery only deepened the fresh wound in her heart—as if her mother had lied to her and her father. "Can we get out of here, please?"

"What?" he stammered. "Get out of here? We're in hiding, remember?"

"Yes, and I don't want to hide here anymore." She lifted her chin, the tears spilling over and streaking down her flushed cheeks. "Take me away from here, Rider. Please."

Nodding, he closed the book and began packing the backpack. "Get your stuff together," he commanded. His gut tight, he knew of one place he could probably take her, but they would need a plane to get there, and he had a feeling she wasn't going to like that anymore than she had liked anything else that had happened since he met her.

EIGHT

Exchanging Places

WELL, this is fun, Rider thought wryly as they approached the same location they had picked the car up from only two days prior. *Going in circles,* he sneered, glancing over at the girl's white knuckles. "Relax," he commanded. "Planes fly all the time," he added, his tone teetering on condescending.

"I don't care. I still hate it." She sighed, opening her door to exit.

Inside, the pair returned the vehicle and left hastily, taking the shuttle to the terminal. Meri had used her phone to purchase tickets for them against his better judgement but arguing with her had proven pointless. Picking them up at the kiosk, he frowned. "You got us first class?" His voice grating, he struggled not to shout. "We're lying low, remember?"

"I don't care," she repeated, pushing her nose into the air. "I told you I didn't want to fly. And I stayed in your ratty hotel. The last thing I'm going to do is fly for three hours surrounded by…" She stopped short, her eyes darting to meet his.

"Surrounded by what?" His hands clenched as he placed them on his hips. "Not accustomed to sharing with commoners, your majesty?"

"Shut up," she bit angrily. Her brow furrowed, she hissed, "Are you sure we have to fly?"

"Yup, pretty sure," he patronized.

"Then we're going first class." She whirled around and surveyed the line of stores. "I'm getting a drink," she tossed over her shoulder as she strutted away towards a bar.

Rider leered at her rear end twitching inside her jeans. He had decided that he liked her, at least well enough to get her between the sheets if he were able; but with that not looking promising, he harbored a strong desire to get on the plane without her. "You shouldn't walk away from me," he said in her ear as he took the stool next to hers.

"I'll have a Manhattan," she informed the barkeeper, ignoring his surliness.

His jaw locked, he glared at her profile. "You're just gonna sit there, huh?"

"Thanks." She accepted the glass, giving the man a small smile. "I'm going to need another shortly."

"You afraid of flying?" The young blond leaned on the bar and grinned at her.

"I'm uncomfortable with it," she admitted quietly, sipping at her drink.

"Don't worry. Ol' Tom's got the cure." He tapped his name badge and walked away.

Spinning in the chair, Rider looked around, longing to order a drink for himself. However, since they had no idea who might be after them, he thought better of it and turned slowly to face the pair when he brought her next round. "Can I get a coke?" he asked in a surprisingly calm tone.

"Sure." Tom smiled. "You want rum or jack…?"

"No. Just the coke." Rider toyed with his hands, cutting his eyes over to see she had almost finished her drink once more. Watching her fish the cherry out of the bottom and bite it off the stem, he leaned over and whispered, "If you don't slow down, I'm going to have to carry you to the gate."

Laughing loudly, Merideth nodded. "If that's the case, don't wake me until we land."

"Yeah," he agreed, running his fingers over the outside of his lips and accepting the iced soda. "Thanks, man."

"Don't mention it." The bartender glanced at the girl and nodded at her silent request.

"Oh, brother." Rider continued to apply his hand to his face in between swallows. Time passed quickly but not before Meri had finished off five more of the beverages. "Can you stand?" he demanded when she got to her feet.

"Yeah." She nodded while giving him a toothy grin.

"Then come on." He offered her his arm, glad they had checked their bags and he only had his backpack to keep up with.

Fortunately, they were boarded as soon as they arrived at the gate and took their seats in the very front of the plane. Sliding his bag under his seat, Rider took the aisle and placed the girl next to the window, where she promptly began testing out positions for sleeping.

Admiring the oversized loungers, he nodded his approval. They would be comfortable, and he had to admit, the idea of not being crammed between two strangers held a certain appeal. Noticing she had passed out before the plane had leveled out, he laughed quietly to himself. *Man, this girl is some piece of work.*

Fishing in his bag for his drawing tablet and pencils when he was able, he took the opportunity to add more to his latest drawing while glancing over at the girl next to him from time to time. Accepting another soft drink from the flight attendant, he noticed that she lingered a moment, studying his drawing and then the girl next to him before moving on to deliver the rest of the passengers' beverages and snacks.

Arriving at the airport in NOLA after almost four hours of flight, Rider put away his supplies and shook the girl next to him by the arm.

"Huh?" she grunted.

"Wake up. We're there," he informed her, amazed at how heavily she slept.

Stretching and adjusting herself, Merideth stood to exit next to him when they were allowed to leave the plane. "I think that was the best flight ever," she boasted, relieved that her plan had worked.

"Well, you're still drunk, so stay close to me," he informed her after hearing her slurred speech. "You must be a light-weight."

"I am not!" she replied angrily. "I don't drink often."

"Exactly." He chortled at her obvious frustration. "When we get to my bike, you're going to have to hang on tight."

"Your bike?" She perked up, appearing to be soberer already. "You don't have a car?"

"Nope." He guided her along the stretches of walkway and down to collect their luggage.

"Then…" Her chest heaved. "How are we getting our suitcases to your house?"

Realizing she was thinking more clearly than it appeared, he chuckled. "Relax. I'm putting you and them in a cab. I'll take my bike and follow along." Doing as he said, he gave the driver the address and sent them on their way, confident he would catch up to them before they could get there.

Inside the taxi, Meri looked around her with wide eyes. The buildings passing by had her in awe—old structures mixed with remolded versions. However, it was the gutted skeletons that shocked her the most. "Is all this from Katrina?" she asked the driver, surprised that it hadn't all been repaired.

"Yup," he informed her casually. "They's still workin' on much of it, but sum of it's been put back t' normal."

Looking out the glass behind her, she caught sight of Rider on a large motorcycle, bringing up the rear. Settling back into the seat, she admired many of the shops that lined the narrow streets and peered up at the balconies above them. "Are those apartments?" She pointed out a set when they stopped at a light.

"Yeah." The driver nodded. "This here's the quarter. Your place is jus' a few streets ova'."

Her heart beating a little faster, she quickly blamed the alcohol for her flutter of excitement. She had never spent time in the South and certainly had never ventured into such a place as this. Her mind drifting, she wondered what it would be like to design replacement décor and help with the reconstruction of the remaining buildings in need of repair.

To her surprise, Rider stood at the curb waiting on them when the cab came to a stop. Taking their bags out of the trunk, he then inspected her as he paid the driver. "How're you feeling?" he inquired, his voice almost tender.

"Better," she breathed, her eyes still taking in her surroundings. "I had no idea what to expect," she informed him, her fingers indicating the building across the street. An empty skeleton, bare framework lay exposed inside of the thick exterior walls, but no signs of current work could be seen—as if it had been gutted and left to rot. "Why did they tear everything out?"

"The structures are protected. They can't demolish them, and they have to meet certain criteria to be rebuilt," he stated matter-of-factly. "Come on. Let's get you settled in." He ushered her inside. Climbing the narrow stairs to the second floor, her left hand trailed the wall in front of him, and he got a good view of the slender ass that made his heart beat faster. *Shit. This woman is going to make me go blind!* he lamented mentally, his fingers tingling at the idea that at any moment, he could reach out and touch the object of his desire.

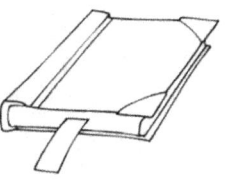

NINE

Hidden Clues

REACHING the top of the stairs, Rider's mind darted to what lay on the other side of his door. His voice tight, he excused himself, brushing against her as he inserted the key and pushed the covering free. Leading the way through the entrance, he placed the suitcases on the floor, anxious to see her reaction when she learned of his secret—one that went much further than sketches in a ragged notebook.

Merideth froze the instant she cleared the door frame, her eyes swinging around to take in the barren living room that oddly reminded her of home. Immediately to her left, the wall she had been gliding her fingers along on the outside made up one side of the grand entrance. This first wall was enough to take her breath away, as large sheets of paper and squares of canvas hung across it, covering it from floor to ceiling with a myriad of projects in various stages of completion.

The far wall filled with a set of French doors, she could see a small seating area out on the balcony, basking in the evening sun. In front of one of the chairs sat an easel, the table next to it holding a collection of brushes. Her eyes flicking to his drawn features for an instant, she followed the line of the room, where the right-hand wall appeared equally covered in scenes similar to those she had passed on their journey from the airport—old buildings, shops, and people.

Noting the hall that led to the rooms at the other end of the apartment, the wall facing the door was missing, replaced by an alcove that made up the kitchen and dining area. "Wow," she breathed, lost in the idea that the table on the tile floor in front of the refrigerator constituted the majority of the furniture in the house, not counting the folding chairs in the living room and patio décor on the balcony.

Pursing his lips, Rider waited for her snide remarks, recalling what a jerk he had been about her New York flat. "I don't bring people here very often," he remarked, sweat beading on his forehead as she silently moved about the room to inspect his work more closely.

Holding her tongue and refusing to ask the obvious question, Meri picked up her suitcase and asked instead, "Do I get a room?"

"S-sure," he stammered, closing the front door and locking it before heading down the hall. Flicking on the light to the bedroom on the right, he glared at the stacks of boxes, books, and painting materials, which covered any furniture that might have been contained there. "Not this one." He grimaced, closing the door and turning to the entrance across the hall.

The second room held a daybed along the left-hand wall and a small dresser against the right, straight in front of the door. Another pair of French doors allowed the sunlight to filter in, illuminating the small space in a warm glow.

Pushing past him, Meri grinned. "Well, at least I can see the floor in this one."

"Yeah," he agreed, removing the stacks of picture frames from the comforter. Dusting at the blanket, he fought to dislodge the odd pieces of debris before she intervened. Lifting it, she shook out the bedding and then glared down at the sheets that had been hidden underneath.

"I guess it's too late for a trip to the laundry," she muttered, annoyed that her accommodations for the night would again be questionable.

"I have a clean set," he offered, turning to the dresser and opening the bottom drawer. Handing her the linens, he left her to return his suitcase to his bedroom, which lay next to hers and formed the furthest corner-to-corner end of the dwelling.

"This is the bathroom." He indicated the remaining door when he returned. "I'm afraid we only have the one, but it's pretty big."

Still adjusting the room to suit her needs, she scowled.

"So, you're an artist?" she accused. "Here I thought you were a manly man, having been in the army and all that."

"I'm as much a man as any other." He stiffened, standing up straighter and squaring his shoulders. "There's nothing wrong with liking to paint!"

"And draw, no less." She snickered before she stood straight up to face him. "No, there isn't." Her eyes bore into him. "Only you don't like to paint. From the looks of this place, you're obsessed with it."

Grinding his teeth, Rider dismissed her with a wave of his hand and clomped out to the kitchen in search of dinner. Having left in a hurry almost a week before, several items in the fridge were tossed, but he soon located enough salvageable items to make a meal. "We'll have to make a trip to the market in the morning," he informed her, watching as she poured herself a glass of his best wine. "Haven't you had enough for one day?"

"I'm under stress." She smiled coyly over the top of her glass. The sun almost set outside, she switched on the overhead light and made the loop once more, only more slowly this time so that she could admire his collection. Moving items so she could see what lay beneath them, she commented aloud, "You have exquisite taste. Your use of color and form are extraordinary."

"Is that one artist to another?" he challenged, unsure if she was genuine.

"Of course." She smiled at him, her hand still holding a few of the pages aside before she dropped them. Lifting his backpack, she removed her mother's book and sat it in the seat of one of the chairs. Seeing his sketchbook, she pulled it out as well. She had peeked through it before, but knowing he took his work more seriously than a casual hobby, she felt the need to inspect it more closely.

Taking the collection of his newest drawings and her mother's text, she opened the sliding door and sank into one of the padded loungers. A yellow bulb glowing above her head, she turned the pages, her fingers tracing the outline and subtle shadows of a few until she reached the end and gasped. Her head jerking around, her eyes fixed on his back as he placed steaks onto plates, and she realized he had the meal completed. Rising quickly, she dropped the fat leather-bound diary in her seat and returned the sketches to his pack before she joined him at the table.

Sitting down to their meal in the kitchen, the pair ate eagerly while they finished off the bottle of wine. She smiled often, and for the first time since he met her, he felt like he would have had a real chance of getting her into bed if he didn't care how he did it. However, morning-after regret wouldn't go over well, especially with her being the daughter of Garrett Monroe. If she had been drinking, she would remain strictly off limits, largely because he didn't fancy prison, or worse, being dealt with by some of those men her father employed for protection.

"You don't say much," he observed once they leaned over their empty plates to sip their beverages and relax.

"What would you like to talk about?" She smiled blissfully.

"I don't know." He chuckled. "You could tell me what you think." He indicated his work with a crooked finger. "You could tell me more about your childhood, about your secretive mother."

"She wasn't secretive," she spat, realizing immediately that in fact, she had been. Shifting anxiously, "All right. My mother preferred her past remain private in a very public life," she agreed.

"We should look at her entry more…or the rest of the book. I know it's painful, but right now, we need to discover who might have killed her and if they will be coming after you," he stated firmly.

Glaring at him, Meri's eyes felt heavy. "Maybe in the morning," she countered while suppressing a yawn. Getting to her feet, she called softly over her shoulder, "Good night, Rider."

Watching her sway down the short section of hallway to her door, the owner of the apartment considered if she meant it or if she was just putting him off with no intention of reading any more of the text. Clearing the table and washing the few dishes, he wiped down the table and placed the tome in the center of it after retrieving it from the balcony chair and securing the doors.

His hand resting on the aged leather, he again felt a tingle of excitement. Something about the book gave his heart flutters, there was no denying. His fingers tingling, he scrunched them into a fist a few times as he ambled off to bed and a night of restless slumber. His dreams haunted by images of old women he had never met, he felt certain they were the authors of the book that now rested in his kitchen waiting to have its mysteries discovered.

Awakened by dim light in a strange place the following morning, Meri left her small quarters to discover Rider already awake and preparing their breakfast. "I thought you were out of food," she stated accusingly, lifting the tome from the table and moving it to a folding chair in the living area so she could set their places.

"It's pretty lean." He chuckled. "Fortunately, eggs last a little longer than most other things."

Spying the bread, she shook her head. "Where did you go?"

"To the little market down the street," he confessed. "I didn't want to wake you, and I was only gone for a few minutes. Besides, I already told you I don't see how anyone could locate us here."

Pursing her lips, she placed plates, glasses, and flatware out for them and took a seat. Sharing the meal in a comfortable silence, only broken by the occasional story or observation, the pair seemed to slowly be reaching a common acceptance of one another. Feeling her trust in him growing, Meri offered, "Do you still want to revisit my mother's entry?"

"Yes, of course." He nodded. "It'll be difficult to decide

our next move if we don't get some clues, and right now, that book is the only one we've got."

Rising, Meri retrieved the book and returned to the table while Rider cleared away their plates and made sure the flat surface had been wiped before placing the heirloom upon it. Opening it again, they inspected the first few pages before he snapped his fingers. "Let me get my laptop. We can finally find out what some of this means."

Grasping the edges, she partially closed the book and lifted it so that he would have room when he returned. When she held it up, a feather fell from the binding and landed in front of her. Laying down the tome, she lifted the soft white plume, her fingers running along the stiff spine.

"What's that?" he asked, adjusting the screen as he reclaimed his seat.

"I don't know." She smiled, toying with the soft spines. "I think it was caught in the binding."

"It was probably between some of the pages…like a bookmark," he observed, plucking it away from her. The moment his fingers touched it, he froze. The tingle he felt the first time he had come in contact with the strange book on Meri's shelf sizzled within him. "Well, isn't this unusual," he observed, turning it so that the small scrape marks along the stiff center could be seen more clearly.

"It was in the binding," she repeated more confidently. "If it had been between pages, we would have discovered it previously—either when you were snooping or when we were looking through the book at the motel."

His eyes shifting to stare into hers, his placid expression gave no hint of the turmoil that raged within him. Licking his lower lip, he laid the feather next to his keyboard and typed *Camden, NJ* into a search bar. A moment later, he selected a lengthy historical briefing and asked, "Shall I read aloud or turn it so we can both see?"

"Let me read it." She claimed the device, turning it and beginning at the top. Leaning back in his chair, he watched as her mouth moved to speak in a clear and succinct manner. Her voice firm, she gasped when she read that Quakers from Ireland had settled the area in 1677. "That's only a decade before the first date in the book," she observed. Taking the text, he located the date they had seen before and confirmed her connection.

Continuing along, her brow furrowed as she read about how the area had been divided up and slowly moved from a farming community to an industrialized zone. When she had finished, she performed a few more searches for phrases out of the text. "This"—she thumped the page—"is Gaelic."

"Gaelic?" he repeated, appearing perplexed.

"Yes." She ran the tip of her finger across one of the lines. "I typed this in, and it brings up a translator. It's like a prayer of some kind." Adjusting the screen, she allowed him to view the results. "Fitting for a Quaker, don't you think?"

Lifting the feather and toying with it gently, he grinned. "Type in part of your mother's. Let's see what she might have been praying for."

TEN

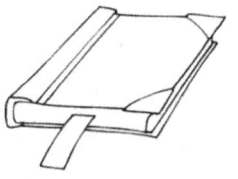

Tandem Wishes

HER FINGERS FLYING TO COMPLY, Merideth licked at her lips anxiously. Having discovered that her mother had been in love with someone else before her father had rocked her hard. Since first learning of the romance, she had considered that giving her the book may have been her mother's way of dealing with the guilt of some torrid affair. Of course, with her mother gone, she had no way to confront the woman over the issue.

Realizing that had put things into perspective for the girl. If her mother hadn't been murdered, she could have done precisely that and found out everything about the man and the passionate love they had shared. With her mother gone, she would have to find her answers in her only remaining source—the family diary. She had a deep fear working its way into her gut that their relationship might be at the root of her mother's death, and that made it all the more important that she discover the truth about dear Teddy.

"It says here," she indicated the first section, "*Peace between the past, the present, and the future.*"

Scribbling the line on a small notepad from the counter that probably held a shopping list most days, Rider grinned. "That's a bit vague. Do another." Lifting the pencil, he glared at the words as if they might rearrange themselves into a more revealing sequence.

Her digits jumping across the keyboard, she inhaled in genuine excitement. "This isn't any better." She tapped the screen. "*May the keeper of joy smile down upon you.*" She grimaced. "This seems pointless. They're just…platitudes."

He nodded, not ready to let it go. "Try one more, at least. Maybe one from the bottom." Scowling at the top of the yellowed page, he could see no date, and therefore had no idea when the stanzas had been written.

"*Through knowledge comes tranquility, understanding, and love.*" She scooted the seat back from the table, causing it to scratch harshly across his tile floor. "I'm done." She threw up her hands. "This isn't getting us anywhere."

Adding the final quote to his list, Rider tapped his writing device against it for a moment, wishing she would continue. "I think it could be important," he finally surmised. "I know it doesn't look like much, but it does give us some insight into your mother's frame of mind."

"Then you do it. I'm getting a shower," she replied crisply as she sauntered down the hall. Retrieving her makeup and fresh underclothes, a pair of shorts, and a lighter top to combat the muggy air, she closed herself into the private space and cranked on the spray.

Listening to her for a moment, Rider grinned to himself. *May the keeper of joy smile down upon you.* It almost sounded like a blessing. *And who are we to judge Ezamay's wishes or where they might lead?* Scooting the screen over closer to him, he started at the top of the lengthy passage and began to type.

Not quite as agile at the task as she had been, he managed to put the entire first stanza in. Once it had been translated, he copied it to a word document instead of writing it down and then moved on to the next. Once he had completed all of Ezamay's pages, he sent it to his printer, located at the back of the apartment in his bedroom, next to the wireless router. Stretching, he noticed that the water had cut off in the shower, and he surmised that she was primping.

Rising, he poured himself a cup of coffee and moved to the balcony to enjoy the mid-morning air. Rider liked his little studio on the edge of the French Quarter. When he came to NOLA, the place had been a disaster, literally. But with long hours and hard work, things had slowly been rebuilt and put back in order, at least for the most part. He had a hand in that renewal, and it did feel as if the keeper of joy smiled upon him.

Drawing and painting had scarcely been a hobby to him before NOLA, but it had become his release, allowing him to deal with the pain he carried with him. He had attended the university so that he could develop that talent and capture the rebirth taking place around him.

The project across the street had captivated him, and he had taken the apartment so he could watch the progress up close. He sketched the building several times through the process, and it was one of his most treasured series of drawings. First, it had been dark, dank, and falling apart, almost a reflection of his inner being after leaving the military. However, once the renovators came and stripped out the interior, it became more like it appeared now.

Then, only a few weeks ago, the latest crew had added some supports on the inside and done a bit of prep work for possibly reconstructing it. *Meri's a designer. I wonder if she could make it look like it did before, if not better.* He had seen her apartment, and he felt certain that she got the same high from creating something beautiful that he did.

The idea of her staying on long enough to take part in the task intrigued him for about half a second before he recalled what happened the last time he had let anyone into his life for more than a few weeks. "Yeah, not going to make that mistake again," he said aloud.

"What mistake?" Meri replied, joining him to admire the view.

Startled, he glanced at her to find her hair dripped onto her fresh powder-blue blouse, causing large wet spots on her shoulder and chest. Her bra clearly visible through the growing dampness, he admired the lace trim that covered her right breast and imagined it would fill his hand perfectly if he were to lay his palm over it.

His pants growing tight in the groin, he shifted to hide his desire and indicated the structure across from them with an open palm. "Just thinking about the mess they made while they were taking it apart," he lied flatly, then shook off the conversation. "What would you like to do today?"

Taking the cushioned chair behind her, Merideth studied him as he towered over her. "You're not a very good liar, Rider," she informed him bluntly. "What mistake? Are you talking about me or something I've done?"

Not daring to look at her, he blinked a few times. "Are you always this nosey? Maybe I was talking to myself, and those words weren't meant for you."

His reply like a slap in the face, she sighed loudly. "Are you always an asshole when you're feeling vulnerable?"

His head instantly pivoting to glare at her, he demanded, "Who says I'm vulnerable?"

Her half-smile toying with him from behind her cup, she considered revealing what she had discovered in his sketchpad the night before. Deciding to hold the information for a later time, she replied, "All men are vulnerable. It's when they feel the need to deny it that it's the most obvious."

Pursing his lips, he shook his head at her, feeling as if he had been baited by a pro. "You're a real head job, you know that?"

Giggling, she lowered her cup and said softly, "I have

no idea what to do next. You brought me here to keep me safe, but we have no way of knowing if it worked. Do we dare to go out? Do we stay locked up in here and getting on each other's nerves?"

"I need to check in with Dad and your father." He nodded absently as if she had suggested it herself. Pulling his phone out of his back pocket, his eyes dropped to stare at her freshly shaved legs, imagining the smoothness they would offer. Her left crossed over the right, she bounced it gently, and without thinking, he reached out to caress the bare thigh about an inch above her knee. Realizing what he had done at the same instant that his father answered the call, he yanked his digits back and stomped through the door.

"Hey, Dad!" he said, his voice two octaves higher than normal.

"Hello," Thaddeus replied. "Don't tell me where you are," he followed up quickly.

"Uh, ok. Has something else happened?" Rider's brow furrowed, and he turned to see that Merideth hung on every word.

"No. We're still piecing things together, with the police doing their part. There's certain things that can't be accounted for, at least for the time being."

"Well, Meri and I may have one of those things," Rider suggested in a quieter tone.

"What?" Thad's voice grew tense. "How?"

"Ezamay had given her three books, like the ones on the

shelf in the den at your place—ancient things with yellowed pages. Someone broke into her apartment and stole two of them, but the third wasn't with the others, and they didn't get it." He grinned at her as he spoke. "This one has stories in it written by different women, some of them in Gaelic. We've translated some of her mother's if you want to hear it."

"Sure." Thad's voice remained tense.

Strutting down the hall, Rider noticed that the girl leapt to her feet to follow. Retrieving the list from his printer, he read from the beginning but only made it halfway through the first stanza before his father cut him off.

"Oh, dear God," Thaddeus grunted. "Rider, listen to me. Under no circumstances do you share that with anyone. I'll find someone you can trust. Just hang tight, and I'll call you back as soon as I have found a tuath to help you."

"A what?" Rider demanded, only hearing silence on the other end. Glaring at the blank screen, he could see that his father had ended the call rather abruptly. Folding the pages, he returned to the kitchen to perform a new search.

"What did he say?" Meri demanded, annoyed that he hadn't filled her in automatically.

Ignoring her, he typed *tuath* into the search bar, his chest growing tight to see *tuatha witch* pop up as one of the auto-complete options. The curser hovering over it for a moment, he heard the girl next to him gasp, and he knew she had seen it. "Well, I guess we're onto something, even if we don't like where it's going." He sighed and pressed the button.

At the top of the page, *Tuatha was a powerful witch from the 18th century. She had been entombed into a cave for two...* appeared.

"That's what your father said?" Merideth asked a bit breathily.

Dropping his left arm around her, he pulled her slender frame against him in a big-brother sort of way. "Don't be scared," he whispered into her hair, himself feeling petrified. Clicking the link, they both stared at it for a long moment before he blurted, "It's a damned TV show!"

The couple laughing hysterically, he glanced at the pages he had dropped on the table while he searched. Lifting them, he again read a few of the lines, not seeing anything incriminating about them. "I don't get it." His chuckles faded. "He said he would find a tuath to help us, and he seemed rather upset."

Going back to the original search, they discovered that *tuath* meant rural people in old Ireland. Reading a few of the passages, they held no reference to anything out of the ordinary. "Maybe I heard him wrong," he admitted quietly.

"I doubt that." Merideth tapped the screen. "It's too big of a coincidence that *tuath* means a person, any kind of a person, in Gaelic—the same language that my ancestors chose to write in. But it does appear to be an innocent reference," she conceded.

Smiling, he nodded at the girl. "Let's get out of here.

I'm sure we've lost whoever is after you. We aren't connected in any way, and there's no reason for them to find us here. I'll take you to lunch," he gushed on, stepping over to close the patio doors and returning to shut down the computer. "I know this great place on Decatur called Bubba Gump. A little touristy, but a great place to eat." Dropping the feather between the pages, he closed the book and shoved it and the translation into his pack. Making a quick call, he requested a taxi for them to ride in comfortably.

"Aren't they like a chain or something?" she countered, slipping on her sandals.

"Yeah, I think they are," he agreed, "but it's still good food." Opening the exit for her, he watched her descend for a moment before he slung the bag over his shoulder and turned to lock the door. He wasn't sure what his dad had been rambling about, but it would work out. In the meantime, he would get another chance at getting Meri out of her clothes, and this time, he planned on keeping her sober while he did it.

ELEVEN

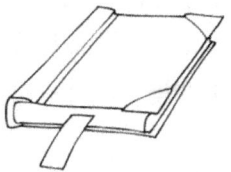

Through the Years

STOPPING at the sidewalk below with a faint smile, Merideth glared up at the sun, which warmed the area to a balmy mid-eighties even in the middle of October. "So different than home," she commented when he joined her.

"How so?" He held his grin easily.

"Oh, just the heat." She chuckled. "It reminds me of being in California, almost. I like the thought of winter back home until I'm in the middle of it, and then"—her laughter tinkled softly—"not so much." Her purse falling down her shoulder, she adjusted the strap. "Now that Mom's gone, I'm not sure that I'll stay there when I'm ready to build my own shop."

Stepping forward to open the door for her on the arriving cab, Rider agreed, "I've been happy here in the more moderate areas. It doesn't get very cold, and it doesn't get very hot, either." Adjusting into the seat, he observed,

"But you'll have to work there a few years before you can strike out on your own, right?"

"Yes," she agreed, watching the crowded streets. "And building my client base there means I'll more than likely stay, even if it is cold." She sighed. "Is it always like this?" She indicated the throngs of people ambling along the sidewalk.

"This is Bourbon Street, so yes. The rest of the city tends to die down, except in summer, and then it's busy all over town." Arriving in front of the eatery, he climbed out and offered her his hand, then tossed his pack over his shoulder.

"Why do you lug that thing around." She indicated the well-worn bag. "Is it like your man purse?" she teased.

"Nope. I need my materials at all times," he supplied, unaffected by the jab. "You never know when something will need to be sketched, and napkins don't really work for that." He laughed softly.

Appreciating his easy sense of humor, she felt a flutter inside her chest. Merideth had a way about her that put most men off in a hurry, and she liked that he seemed unaffected by her dominant personality. Moving from the air-conditioned taxi to the cool shade of the building, she almost wished she could forget about why they were there. Dropping her handbag onto the bench, she slid into the hardwood seat and observed all of the decorations, which centered around the movie *Forrest Gump*.

"They really did their homework," she observed, picking up on the details in the items hanging on the wall.

"Yeah," he agreed. "I think it's the artistic side that allows us to appreciate it." He grinned.

Letting down her guard, Meri felt at ease. "I've always had that part of me…that needed to be fed and set free. I spent ages perfecting my dollhouses when I was a child. They still decorate my bedroom in my parents' house, but they don't bring near the joy that they used to." She recalled waking up surrounded by them only a few mornings before.

"You have bigger pads to deal with," he observed.

"Yes, and bigger clients than Barbie," she sneered. "Honestly, I think you would have been doing me a favor if you had gotten me kicked off that project in Williamsburg."

"Oh?" He picked at the hush puppies that had been set before him.

"Oh, yes." She stared at the table before her. "Some people just don't appreciate those who work for them."

"Yeah, I get that. I'm glad I don't really have a boss anymore," he observed.

Looking up at him, she became intrigued. "You don't have a job?"

"Nope." He shook his head. "I do volunteer work—helping the homeless, working on restoration projects, maybe a few odd jobs here and there, but other than that, I draw and paint. Period."

"Wow, that must be nice," she conceded, realizing that

being that type of artist held its advantages. "It's hard to be a decorator without a client to decorate for."

"I'm sure there are jobs out there if you were to know where to look." He lifted his arms as their plates were placed on the table. "When we're done here, I'll take you on a little tour, if your feet can take it in those sandals. Show you around the quarter a bit."

"Ok." She nodded, excited to visit the places she had heard about many times from others but had never had the chance to see for herself.

Lingering over their meal, each of them exchanged stories from their childhoods, and she learned that Rider had not only been his father's only child, they had lost his mother when he was very young.

"I don't really remember her," he admitted quietly. "It's just always been me and Dad."

"That's sad," she agreed, picking up on his somber mood.

"It's ok," he countered, accepting his change from the waitress. "Let's get out of here."

Outside, the sun shone brightly above them, and they meandered down the walk. Stopping at the occasional shop, Meri found herself more drawn to the balconies above many of the buildings and the furnishings that decorated them than anything the shops were selling inside. Stopping outside one in particular, she scrutinized the molding that ran up the front, from ground to roof. "This is exquisite," she breathed.

"The French Quarter isn't really French anymore," he informed her. "It's been through numerous periods of addition and transition. It's still breathtaking, though."

"Yes. I could see from your living room that you love to draw it," she agreed, giving him a quick glance to see that he watched her every move. Lifting her foot, she ran her hand down to caress her ankle. "Damn, I'm getting a blister. These aren't the best shoes for sight-seeing, I guess."

"No worries." He chuckled, pulling out his phone. "Hey, Mac," he called into the device. Giving the man on the other end their location, he hung up with a mysterious grin. "I used to ride for one of the bike-cabs around here. One of them is going to pick us up and take us the rest of the way."

Eyeing him suspiciously, she hadn't realized that he had a particular destination in mind. When the cab arrived, she laughed at its odd construction, a bright yellow cart with a single bench seat covered by a roof. In front of that, a bicycle was attached, where a slender man with large calves worked to haul them along.

"You used to do this?" She giggled at the thought of his large frame seated on the narrow bike and fighting for momentum.

"Yeah. It was great. I made good money and stayed in shape." He patted his belly firmly.

Cutting her eyes over, she gazed at him out of the corner before facing him squarely. "Is this really your job?" She indicated the man in front of them. *Had he lied to her in a roundabout way?*

"*Was*...my job," he emphasized the past tense firmly. "It's been a couple of years since I needed the income, but I guess I could always fall back on it if I needed to."

Her head bobbing back and forth with the sway of the cart, Meri let the subject drop, not certain that she could believe what he told her. Mysteries abounded where Rider Bradshaw was concerned, and she had to admit he had drawn her in. She might not be interested in a long term relationship, but the idea of a hot and heavy physical one had begun to make her sweat in all the right places.

Arriving at a large, glass-front structure, the couple climbed out of the contraption, and Rider handed the man a large bill. "Can you be back here in say...an hour?"

"Sure," the taxi replied. "One, two, just say when. Or, better yet, let me give you my card with my direct line." He fished it out of his pack on the back of the cab, along with a bottle of water. Handing the small piece of card stock to her companion, he pointed at the number. "That's my cell. Just give me a buzz when you're ready for a pick-up, and I'll be right here."

"Thanks." Rider shoved the card into his pocket and indicated the door of the building behind them to the girl. "This way, madam."

Smiling at his tone and the guiding hand he placed on her back, Merideth leaned against him and allowed him to take charge. Inside, the cool air surrounded them, a sharp contrast to the growing heat outside. Her eyes roving over the rows of shelves, she quickly realized they were inside a gallery.

"Oh my God," she breathed, noticing the unique *Rider* etched into the corners of a few of the paintings. "These are yours," she observed softly.

"Yeah." He grinned broadly. "This is my studio—the public one. Me and a few other guys sell our stuff through here." He indicated the clerk who had not interrupted them. Following her, he watched as her expression grew more enthralled. When she paused in front of the collection of sketches of his favorite subject—the building across from his apartment—his chest grew tight. "Recognize it?"

"Of course," she replied airily. "It's like a dream, with such detail, but magical and lost once you awaken."

Chuckling, he left her to admire them. "I'm not sure I would go that far," he tossed over his shoulder as he headed towards the offices in the back.

Alone with his work, she moved slowly through the rows, unsure how long it took him to produce so many incredible pieces of work. *Obviously, he's quick at it,* she thought as she recalled the sketch in the back of his book. *He's finished that one in only a few hours.* It had to have been only a few since she had never actually seen him working on it.

Ready to leave a while later, Rider made the call that would deliver them to another restaurant for a cozy dinner, this time in a darker setting and lights down low. Snuggling into a round booth, he sat beside her, allowing him to seductively touch her from time to time.

Walking beside him afterwards, as they strolled gently towards his home in the next block, Meri sighed wistfully. Her hand in his, their fingers entwined, she could feel the pull of him upon her. "Do you ever have…friend sex?" she asked coyly.

"Sure." He chuckled. "I'm not really boyfriend material, but I do like an occasional roll in the hay." He grinned down at her. "Are you thinking about making a night of it?" He stopped walking and pulled her around to face him.

Her heart pounding, Merideth's breath grew shallow. Raising her mouth to meet his, she tasted his lips, the salty sweat of the day teasing her. "You won't get the wrong idea about me, will you?" she quarried in a shaky voice, her hand pushed hard against his muscled chest. She could feel his lump pressing against her belly before he undulated to push against her in a playful manner.

"You're not teasing me, are you?" he asked hoarsely.

"No. I'm not a tease," she informed him firmly. "When we get back to your place, I think we're going to pull an all-nighter," she informed him with a growl.

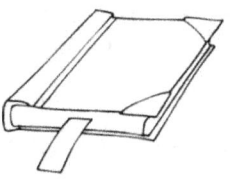

TWELVE

Happenstance

CLIMBING the stairs arm in arm, Rider's groin ached. He couldn't believe how well their day had gone or that she had come around so quickly. Pausing at the door, she stepped onto the top and turned to face him. Still taller, but not by as much, he grinned at her before she lifted her mouth to kiss him.

"Meri," he breathed.

Parting her lips, her hands roamed over his chest, then around to his back, where they were blocked by the backpack he had insisted on carrying around all day. "Take me to bed," she groaned.

"Absolutely," he replied, fishing out his key and freeing the lock.

The apartment dim as they entered, she continued to fondle him as he dropped their bags by the door, closing it heavily and locking it. Not bothering with the lights, he pushed her towards the back of the house. "Friend sex," he mumbled.

"Yes," she agreed, pausing when she heard paper crunching beneath her feet. The walls of his home may have been covered in drawings and paintings, but the floors had been clear. Looking down, she could see the outline of trash and unidentifiable debris strewn about. "Rider," she stated urgently.

"Yeah, baby?" He pressed against her, undeterred at her pause. "You don't like beds?" he asked, urging her to move on down the hall.

Staring at the kitchen, her eyes adjusting to the darkness, she could make out the overturned table and computer on the floor. "Rider, someone's been here!" her voice grew loud.

Releasing her, his eyes darted around, and he kicked a few of the items at their feet. "Shit!"

Taking her hand, he pulled her towards the door and flicked on the light. The room in chaos, much as her apartment had been only a few days before, he looked around the walls at his paintings. Many of them had been vandalized, having graffiti sprayed across them, and many more had been pulled down and littered the floor. "Oh, man," he groaned, turning slowly to take it all in before heading down the hall.

"Put on your jeans and regular shoes," he instructed as he reached the door to his room.

"What? Why?" she demanded, unable to hide the tremor in her voice.

"We're getting out of here," he said in a deliberate tone. "We have to get further away from who we are." Opening his suitcase, he asked, "Do you have another pair of jeans or just those?"

"I only brought the one pair," she informed him, sliding her legs in and buttoning the waist.

"Then grab a couple of tops and put them in here. A few changes of underclothes and that's it," he said as he did the same.

"What about the rest?" She sniffed, disturbed that they had been running for days but weren't getting anywhere.

"We'll have to strap the bag to the back of my bike, so we have to travel light." He shoved her things in for her and carried it to the living room. Taking the backpack and her purse, he laid them in the top and zipped everything into one bundle. Then lifting a heavy leather jacket off the row of hooks behind the door, he handed it to her. "Put this on," he instructed.

"It's too warm for this," she protested as he helped her hands into the sleeves.

"Not for long," he informed her solemnly as he donned his own. "Let's go."

Mounting the motorcycle a few minutes later, the pair of them rode through the darkness. Terrified, Merideth leaned against him, her fingers clutching his shoulders as he maneuvered them through the streets. Arriving across town a short while later, he parked the bike among a group of others outside a bar.

"We're going in here?" She sounded doubtful. It was only about ten, but the place looked rough and far beyond her comfort zone, even with him to protect her. Watching with wide eyes, she shifted anxiously as he unstrapped their combined suitcase.

"No." He took her hand, his eyes ever watchful around them. "I know a place we can spend the night." Leading her between the buildings, they turned at the alley and followed it for a few blocks. Arriving at a large storm drain, he held her hand firmly and helped her down the incline. Sensing her distrust of the shadows beneath the bridge before them, he pulled her towards it and growled, "It's ok. A community of homeless lives down here."

"Oh, and how do you know that?" she hissed, forcing him to wait until her eyes had adjusted and she could see better.

"I live here, remember?" he bit tensely. "I do volunteer work with a soup kitchen. I know some of these people."

As soon as she could make out the smooth walls, she noticed that a few large lumps did indeed lie at the base of them, presumably men wrapped in sleeping bags. Allowing him to guide her, they made their way through the tunnel, where some of the inhabitants were awake, talking to each other and watching the couple as they passed by. Meri's heart pounded with every step, her mind racing in disbelief at the twist of fate that had brought them to such an appalling place.

Eventually finding the other end, they came out into a clearing, with steep walls running up the side where they had exited. Before them lay a group of dense trees and underbrush, and in the center stood a large barrel with a fire burning inside of it, where the inhabitants could warm themselves if they needed to. "Relax," he instructed, holding her firmly. "They aren't going to hurt us, and we can hide among them, at least for tonight, and get some sleep."

Clutching his oversized jacket around her, she moved stiffly beside him, thankful he had thought to put it on her before they left. Making it through the open area and collection of dirty and ragged beings, she followed as he made his way into the line of trees. Finding more people curled at the bases of some of them, they kept moving until they came to a spot that appeared to suit him.

"Take this one," he instructed, dropping the bag and pushing her to sit in the arch of the large roots. Like a large basin, the soft earth beneath her, she leaned against the hard wood and shivered. Kneeling down and working himself in next to her, he pulled her against his chest, her breasts pressed against him. His arms sliding beneath the jacket, he pulled her snuggly to him, essentially using her and the coat as a blanket. "So much for friend sex," he muttered.

Meri would have laughed at the comment if she hadn't

been so petrified. "You actually expect me to sleep here?" she hissed, her eyes moving to keep watch around them.

"It's ok. We're safe," he insisted. "Nothing to worry about." His chin resting on top of her head, he forced his breathing to slow. His palm tracing the line of her back in a slow, comforting circle, he waited for her to drop off first before he allowed his own eyes to close so that sleep could find him.

The following morning, a thick fog hung along the ground, obstructing their view. Stiff, Rider shifted and groaned. "Meri," he whispered, relieved to feel the lump of her as she still lay against him, breathing deeply. Giving her a shake, he then pushed her so that he could sit up from his prone position.

Her eyes fluttering open as he moved her, the girl gasped at the wisps of white water vapor that hung over them. "I can't believe I fell asleep!" she observed in a quiet tone.

"You've had an exciting week," he recalled, getting to his feet. As soon as she stood beside him, he swung his gaze around, observing that the fog only reached mid-thigh, and they could see clearly over the top of it, but the ground below would be dangerous to transverse. "We have to be careful," he acknowledged the situation. "We don't want to trip over anything on the way out."

Locating their bag beside his feet, he held it in one hand and her fingers in the other. Guiding her along, they again passed small clumps of people who only watched as they departed. Climbing the storm drain a bit more difficult than coming down it, she grunted. "I can't believe we slept out here in the open."

"What, you never went camping?" He chortled quietly.

"No," she bit cleanly. "Never in my life."

Looking around at the entrance to the alley, Rider nodded. "It's ok. I'm sure you're about to experience a whole lot of things you've never done before," he informed her grimly. Arriving at the bike a few minutes later, he attached the bag with his bungee cords and placed her on the back. Climbing on himself, he kicked over the engine and they rolled away in search of breakfast and a place they could make a call to find out what they should do next.

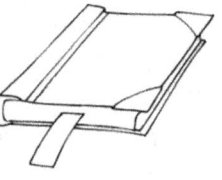

THIRTEEN

Expected

SITTING IN A SMALL DINER, Rider grinned at her. "You've got dirt on your face," he informed her with a chuckle, indicating the smudge using his own as a mirror.

Wiping at it, a tear spilled over and streaked her cheek, and she sniffled loudly.

"Hey." He sat up straighter, taking her hand across the table and massaging it. "It's ok," he soothed.

"No, it isn't. It hasn't been ok in days or weeks," she said with a trembling jaw, "or maybe even months. Somehow, I feel like all of this is my fault," she confessed.

"Your fault?" He appeared stunned. "How would any of this be your fault?"

"I didn't do what was expected of me," she sniveled. "All my mother wanted was a few grandbabies. Is that too much to ask?"

His jaw wide, he stammered, "Are you serious? You think all of this happened because you don't have any kids?"

"I think that it is." She toyed with her spoon, placing it into her cup of coffee and stirring it anxiously. "I had a dream last night—about a witch who's chasing us."

"A witch!" his voice grew loud, and he glanced around quickly to see who might be watching them. "Merideth, you only dreamed that because of the *tuath*. Because of that TV show we found when we searched for it. It isn't real," he reassured her in as strong a voice as he could muster.

Shivering, she sipped from her cup. Unnerved, she could feel her heart pounding and wondered if it was loud enough that he could hear it as well. *Why couldn't we have spent the night making love?* she lamented. *Why is this happening to us?*

The dream had terrified her, and the fact that he made light of it did not resolve the issue. "We need to call your father," she pushed. "You find out from him what he was talking about and see if he knows anyone who can help us."

Trying his phone, he frowned. "It's dead." He sighed, opening the suitcase in the seat beside him and digging farther into his backpack hidden inside it. Pulling out his charger and back-up battery, he sighed. "This will get me about half a battery, but I really need to plug it in so we can get a good charge. We have no idea how long it will be before we can do it again."

Using the cord to connect the small box, he laid them on the table and indicated the waitress. "Here comes our food. Take your time and enjoy your meal," he said quietly.

Meri could see the darkness in his features and wondered what he might be hiding from her. Scooting her eggs around with a fork, she ate at them slowly. Crunching the toast, she felt somewhat warmer inside. While they were enjoying the meal, she looked around at the walls. "There has to be a place somewhere that we can charge every-thing," she stated more calmly, aware that her own phone was dead as well.

Catching their server's attention, Rider asked, "Is there a place she can charge her phone?"

Staring at the couple with wide eyes, the young woman appeared surprised for a moment before stepping back and peering under the tables on either side of them. "There's an outlet under this table." She pointed at the one behind him. "You're welcome to move if you want to use it," she said as she observed his open suitcase next to him.

"Thanks." He grinned at her, indicating for Meri to take her food and change seats. Moving to obey, she complied with a hot flush staining her cheeks.

"She probably wonders if we stole them," she hissed when he joined her, inserting two plugs and connecting both their devices.

"I'm sure that she does," he agreed, looking around them again anxiously. Something about her dream had put him on edge, even if he had dismissed it aloud. "We'll give it as long as we can and make the call when we leave." Determined to put her mind at ease as it had been yesterday when they talked about their childhoods, dreams, and futures, he changed the subject.

Met with stiff silence, Rider could see that their rapport had been broken. "Baby, you need to relax," he informed her softly. "This is going to work out." He flicked her a brief smile.

"It's hard," she whispered back, again on the verge of tears. "I'm not like this, Rider. Sleeping under trees and eating at greasy dives. You may be ok with this, but this isn't me."

Stunned, he grimaced. "I'm not going to argue with you about this. We can talk about it later when we're not so exposed."

Rolling her eyes, she looked away, her gaze drawn to the counter where an old woman sat eating breakfast. Her clothing tattered and frayed, she could easily have been one of the drifters who had shared their sleeping quarters. Finished with her meal, she stood and excused herself in a quiet tone. "I'll be back." Locating the bathrooms at the back of the café, she went inside and removed as much of her clothing as she dared.

At least the water's warm, she lamented as she applied it to her delicate skin. Using a few of the paper towels, she dried herself as gently as she could, uncomfortable with the roughness of them against her flesh. *This isn't camping,* she fumed. *This is ludicrous.* Her jaw set, she ran her fingers through her hair and picked out bits of leaves and twigs that she had collected during the night.

Finally presentable and feeling moderately better, she returned to their table while holding her head up. "Are we all charged?"

"Not yet." He indicated her seat. "A bit longer should do it." He smiled at her efforts. "I'm sorry all of this has happened," he whispered when she had settled in to wait with him. "If we could change it, we would, but at this point, we just have to deal with it and not let it beat us."

"I know." She sighed. "I'll do what I have to do, Rider. I promise."

The pair waited for their phones to be recharged and then gathered their things, taking care to ensure that nothing had been left behind. They were down to a single bag of possessions and couldn't afford to lose anything else at the moment.

Outside, Rider turned on his device and dialed his father anxiously. Moving down the walk, he paused against the wall and waited. "Dad?" he demanded when the call was answered.

"Yes," the senior Bradshaw replied from the other end, his voice sounding strained.

"I can't talk long," Rider informed him. "There's been more trouble, and we hope you can give us something —anything."

"I've found someone," Thad stated in monotone. "A

tuath that can help you. Let me give you an address, and you should go there straight away."

"Ok." His son flipped open his notepad and clicked his retractable pen. "Give it to me." Jotting down the number and street, he grinned. "Thanks, Dad. I know this place and can take it from here."

"Call when you're able," his father replied and disconnected the line.

Looking back, Rider stared at the diner from which they had just come. Shuffling out the door, the old woman from the counter made her way towards them. His breath tight in his chest, he waited for her to pass, but she didn't. Stopping in front of him, she stared up at Rider, then shifted her beady gaze to the girl. "Are you in trouble, son?" she asked in a hoarse whisper.

Rider stared into her clear blue eyes, his phone still resting in his open palm. A sick feeling washed over him, a damp chill despite the growing warmth of the day. "Do I know you?" he asked softly, curling his fingers around the device and slipping it into his pocket.

Shifting from one foot to the other nervously, Merideth watched the exchange before blurting, "We're fine. Thank you." Seizing his arm, she pulled the man next to her in the direction of his bike, where he repacked their gear. Climbing on and glancing down the street, she could see the old woman had gone. Exhaling loudly, her fingers found their place on his shoulders, and she held on firmly while he steered the way to the location the elder Bradshaw had indicated that they should visit.

Parking in front, he killed the engine and grinned. "This is a shotgun house."

"I'm familiar," she replied, noting the aged architecture and recalling that it would be one room wide, with no hallway between the connected rooms. Under normal circumstances, she might have enjoyed the visit, but today, her nerves were too frayed for pleasure. "Let's get this done, please," she begged.

Guiding her up the sidewalk and mounting the steps, Rider rapped quietly on the screen door. The temperature moderate in the shade of the porch and the large trees in the front yard, he glanced around them with a slight smile. They both would have enjoyed the visit had things been different.

"Hello," a tall, slender woman with fire-red hair greeted them, cup towel in hand. Dropping it onto her shoulder and pushing on the entrance to welcome them, she bade them to step inside.

Hesitant, Rider entered first, holding their single bag in front of him while Merideth followed behind. The front room clean and comfortable, it held dated flower-print furniture with wooden claw feet. The hardwood floor shone brightly as if it had recently been polished, and no dust could be seen on any of the smooth surfaces.

"Your home is lovely," Meri muttered, remembering her manners.

Removing her apron, the woman smiled. "Thank you. Thaddeus said you've had a bad week. Come. Let's see what we can do."

Tearing his eyes away from the immaculate setting, Rider followed the woman into the next room while his companion continued to bring up the rear. The second room a dining area, a large table took up most of the space. Glancing around, this room also appeared freshly cleaned, as did what he could see of the kitchen through the door that lay beyond.

"Let's sit here." The woman indicated the stiff wooden chairs that surrounded the darkly stained surface. Obeying, the couple each took a seat next to the window on the right-hand wall, their baggage on the floor between them.

Settled into their chairs, Meri folded her hands into her lap. "We hope that you can tell us what is going on," she stated without preamble, her features expressionless.

"Yes, I'm sure that would set your mind at ease," their host began.

"Are you a tuath?" Rider cut her off.

Hiding her smile unsuccessfully, the woman agreed, "I am a tuath. My name is Eva," she supplied.

"Good." He grinned back at her. "What does that mean exactly?"

Her eyes shifting back and forth between them, she licked her lips for a moment, then replied, "It means that I have certain connections to ancient traditions."

"You're a witch," Meri blurted, breathless with fear.

Without batting an eye, the woman nodded. "I am. Although we seldom refer to ourselves as such. Many centuries ago, the catholic church did everything within their power to remove every evidence of us from existence, and only those of direct descent have knowledge of us and the power we possess."

The words *direct descent* resonated in Merideth's thoughts, and she subconsciously looked down at the bag that held her mother's ancient diary.

Following her gaze, Rider considered the contents of their remaining possession as well, and then offered, "We have something that might help." Reaching to unzip the suitcase, he lifted out his backpack and laid it on the table before him.

Rummaging inside, he brought out the sketchbook and the old tome, laying it in the center of the table. Pushing the bag and his work aside, he laid the pages of translations on top in case they needed them any time soon.

Catching the edge of the leather binding, their hostess ran her fingers across it lightly. "This is a magical book," she breathed. "It has seen many years in the hands of the tuath."

Holding her tongue, Meri sniffed loudly, on the verge of tears. Leaning towards her, Rider dropped his arm around her in a comforting manner. Her eyes darting up to watch the pair for a moment, Eva's mouth twitched into a slight grin before falling back into unreadable nothingness.

Opening the book, she flipped through the pages,

running her fingers over them lightly from time to time. Her eyes moving quickly, emotions randomly played across her features. "This is a book of spells," she agreed with her previous statement. "Whoever hunts you knows that you have it."

"Why!" Meri gasped.

Raising her gaze to study the girl for a moment, the older woman's voice remained calm. "That, I cannot say. To discover the secrets, you must return to the source."

"The source." Rider scoffed, annoyed at her calm avoidance of real information.

Turning more pages, Eva ignored his indignation, pausing when the page opened to the white feather. Taking it gently, she lifted it, touching the soft stems lightly with her other hand and smiling. "I see." Looking up at the couple across from her, she laid it to the side and continued until she had reached the end.

Reading over Ezamay's words, she continued to smile. Her lips moving slightly, she spoke them in a low whisper, causing Rider's heart to flutter.

"We have them translated," he offered, indicating the folded sheaf of pages.

"That will not be necessary." She grinned more fully, exposing her clean, white teeth. "You must return to your roots and follow the path. When you have visited the resting place of your line, you will see the truth, and you will discover how to protect that which is sacred."

Laying the feather between the yellowed pages, she closed the text and shoved it across the smooth surface. "I hope that helps," she stated warmly as she got to her feet.

"That's it?" Meri snapped. "Where is this place you want us to go? Please"—her lip quivered—"stop talking in riddles and just tell us what to do."

Turning her back, the woman ignored her request and moved towards the kitchen.

"I think we have to go back to New Jersey," Rider surmised. "That's the source of all of this." He indicated the book before them. "Your family in Camden."

Rocking her jaw slightly, Merideth felt strong waves of emotion tearing through her—anger that her life had been disrupted in such a way, fear that someone was looking for them and wanted to take away her mother's gift…or worse. Pushing back her chair, she stomped around the table and entered the modest kitchen to find their host once more donned her apron and stood at the sink, washing dishes.

"What else do you know?" she demanded in an authoritative voice. "You can't insinuate that my mother was a witch and then walk away."

"I have insinuated nothing." The older woman continued with her chore. "I have stated the truth. Your line cannot be chosen. Fate has made you who you are. Follow the path and discover what you must."

Moving up behind her, suitcase in hand, Rider's fingers grasped Merideth firmly by the arm. "Let's go," he whispered. "She's told us all that she's going to, and I don't want to stay here any longer." Pulling her through the door, he turned her towards the exit, and they made their way out to their transportation in silence.

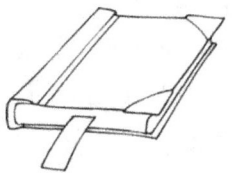

FOURTEEN

Breach of Contract

TAKING A FEW SIDE STREETS, Rider put them onto a highway and rode for several miles before he pulled off to park outside a busy chain restaurant. "We need to eat," he informed her flatly, "and formulate our plan."

Reluctantly, she agreed. "Do we have to keep lugging that thing around?" she indicated the suitcase he had once again unstrapped. "We look ridiculous carrying it in and out with us," she pointed out angrily.

"Fine." He unzipped the bag, pulling out his backpack and handing her the small purse. "We can leave the suitcase, but if someone steals your panties, I don't want to hear any complaints." He snickered. Reattaching the lightened luggage to the bike, he put the bag containing her mother's book over his shoulder and indicated the entrance. "Let's go."

Meri removed the heavy leather jacket once more,

carrying it in front of her. She could go without anything in the bag at the moment, but keeping the wind off of her when they rode was a must. Following obediently, she had grown weary of their ordeal and knew she would do whatever it took to get her life back, and the sooner the better.

Taking their seats after a short wait, the young woman looked around at the décor and then said softly, "Thank you."

"For?" He studied the menu, not looking at her directly.

Blinking back tears, her voice shook. "For bringing me to a nicer place to eat."

His mouth open as he lowered the plastic coated card, he felt unsure how to respond. Nodding slightly, he made an attempt at consoling her. "I know this has all been hard on you. I want to ensure your safety and take care of you, just like I promised I would do."

"I know." She swiped at an escaped tear and pursed her lips. "You're a good man, Rider. Better than I judged you to be when we met."

"You let the ponytail fool you, huh?" He chuckled.

Breaking into an earnest grin, she agreed, "Yes, you really did a number on me. But it's ok. We can go back to Camden and find whatever it is we're supposed to know. Then we can deal with whoever is after us."

Shifting his gaze back to selecting his meal, he sighed. "I hope it's that easy. I've had a bad feeling since we met that you and I were related, and Miss Eva only served to make me suspect it even more."

Her eyes wide, Merideth gasped. "You can't be serious! You think we could be...siblings?" She didn't dare admit the idea had also crossed her mind.

"Or cousins, or anything, really. Camden isn't a very big place, and if both of our families have been there for centuries, it stands to reason that our bloodlines have mingled at some point. Besides"—his voice grew softer—"I guess you failed to notice that if Eva is a witch, and your mother is a witch, that means my father is as well."

"Oh my God!" she breathed, trying to match his calm. "You don't seem that upset about it." Changing the subject, she squirmed. "I can't decide. Get me whatever your having," she said as she dropped her menu back on the table in disgust.

"What's there to be upset about?" he countered, raising his chin at the approaching waitress. "We'll have two steaks, medium rare, steamed veggies, and salads with ranch on the side, please," he informed her as he handed her the menus. Once she had moved on, he continued. "Meri, things are what they are. We can't change our parents or our histories. All we can do is deal with them and hopefully get whoever is after you off your back."

"Let's give them the book," she blurted, wringing her napkin as she said it.

"What?" his voice caught an angry tone. "We can't do that! That would be like...breach of contract. Your mother gave you that book, as if you were meant to keep it safe. If you hand it over, then you've let her down. Besides, since we don't know why they want it, we have no way of knowing what kind of danger that would pose."

Clicking her tongue, she instantly knew he was right. "So you really believe in all the hocus-pocus magical humbo-jumbo?" She tried to play off his accusatory rant.

Studying her for a long moment, he ran his fingers around the outside of his mouth and massaged his thickening stubble. Finally, he acquiesced, "I find it interesting. I'm not saying that I believe in it, but I can't deny the possibility. I've seen some strange things in my life, and finding out that my father is connected to the craft makes a few of them a lot more understandable."

Staring at the centerpiece, Merideth sighed, her shoulders lifting in an exaggerated manner. "I'm tired," she admitted quietly. "There was nothing in my past or my mother's that would indicate any of this—no strange events, no unsavory characters. My life has been extraordinarily ordinary. I miss her," she finished hardly above a whisper.

Taking her hand across the fine linen cloth, Rider gave her a squeeze. "Let's set a few things straight," he said firmly. "First off, I'm going to get to the bottom of the whole blood relation scenario." His mouth twisted into a wry grin. "You still owe me some friend sex, and I intend to collect."

Her face crinkled, she laughed, the spasm growing uncontrollable for a moment as she squinted at him. "Thanks," she agreed, calming herself but holding the smile. "I hope you're not too angry if I decide not to pay up."

"No." He shook his head slightly. "I won't be too angry. We need to get back to Jersey, though. We'll go to the airport, and you can get us tickets. You can even pick first class again if you like, but I don't want you to get all sauced this time."

Anxious, she pulled her hand away and made room for their plates. Her mouth salivating at the sight of the meal, she fought to remain civilized as she cut the meat and shoved bites into her mouth in rapid succession. When she grew tired of chewing, she drank a large portion of her tea and then stated matter-of-factly, "I'll do as you ask. I won't like it, and I warn you, there may be trouble once we get in the air, but I'll try it your way."

"Good." He bounced his fork for a moment. "When we get there, we can start with my old neighborhood. I think it's safe to assume that your mother once lived there as well."

"I think we need to visit the cemetery," she countered, gulping more tea.

"Why would we go there?" He glared at her dubiously.

"Eva said the resting place of my line," Meri replied softly. "The last time I checked, the resting place of all people is ultimately a graveyard."

Curling his tongue, Rider scowled. He hadn't thought of that, and the idea of it sent pure terror coursing through him. All the talk about witches and spells was disconcerting enough, but the idea of walking among their graves, perhaps searching for them, was enough to put is hair on end;

witches were bad news, even if they were related to the mild and meek girl who sat across from him.

Finishing their meal, the couple left the restaurant with full bellies and renewed spirits. Taking the girl's hand as they crossed the parking lot, he toyed with her fingers lightly, wishing they had met under different circumstances. Placing their bags into the suitcase when they arrived back at the bike, he felt glad that nothing appeared to have been touched.

Donning the jacket, Meri climbed on behind him and braced herself for the ride to the airport. Each trip built her confidence ever so slightly, and she still held him in her grip but no longer feared plunging to her death at any moment. Arriving at the busy transportation hub, she accepted her purse and announced, "Ok, I'll get the tickets. Are you calling your father now?"

"Yes," he agreed, pulling out his phone as they walked towards the terminal. Watching her as she headed inside, he called after her, "Come back out here when you've got them."

Giving him a small wave over her shoulder, Merideth followed the crowd and located a ticket counter. Standing in line, she waited anxiously as her eyes darted around her, watching for anyone who might be spying on her.

Outside, Rider's hand shook as he made the call. He liked Meri and needed to know more about their family histories if he were to have any hope of sorting out which compartment in his life that she would fit most neatly into.

"Dad," he stated harshly when the rings finally ceased. "Are you there?" he demanded with a snort.

"I'm here," Thaddeus replied. "Was Eva not able to help?"

"Oh, she helped. We're heading to the source." He chuckled. "And that's what we need to discuss."

"I'm not where I can speak openly," his father stated in a lower tone.

"Then go outside or change rooms. Hell, go visit the john, but you and I need to have this out, right now!" Rider hissed.

His words hesitant, Thad fished, "What's the matter, son? You sound upset. What else has happened?"

Running his fingers over the top of his head, Rider smoothed at his hair. "I just need to know who she is, Dad," he stated in a calmer voice. "No more games. Is she my sister?"

"Your sister!" the older man practically shouted, breaking into a loud rolling laugh. "No, son, she's not your sister, or even related to you for that matter. Her mother and I were friends. More than friends if I dared to be honest. But our families were sworn enemies and had been for centuries. After I lost your mother, Ezamay and I spent a few months together, but when her parents found out, she was banished from our community."

"Jesus." Rider sighed, a flood of relief adding to his tremor. "Are you sure about that? I mean…" he stammered.

"I'm sure," Thad stated emphatically. "Almost Romeo

and Juliet, we were, if we had been young and foolish enough. While we were together, we joked about our love being the catalyst that would put an end to their feud." He sighed. "The truth is it didn't and, in some ways, only made it worse."

Seeing Meri exit the sliding glass doors, Rider turned his back on her. "I have to go. Thank you for the insight." Ending the call briskly, he waited for her to join him with his heart beating like at any moment it would leap out of his chest.

FIFTEEN

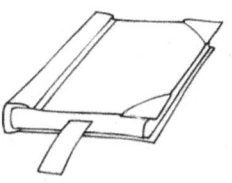

Implied Truth

MERI COULD TELL something was bothering him the moment he turned around. "What's the matter?" she demanded with a frown, unsure she really wanted to know.

"We're not related," he stated flatly, accepting his ticket from her to inspect it. Noting they had less than an hour, he indicated the doors. Sighing loudly, he knew she was entitled to the truth, as far as he could go with it. "Our families hate each other. Your mother was banished from the community after their affair was discovered."

"Affair!" she breathed, her head spinning. "Your father is Teddy, isn't he!"

"He didn't say that." Rider squirmed, picking up their bag and marching towards the entrance. "But he implied as much. He said they were lovers after he lost my mother," he supplied, keeping his eyes on the path before them. "I think we can carry this bag on." He changed the subject and hoped the discussion would die quietly. Leading her through security, he held their conversation at bay as long as he could, but eventually their eyes met, and he knew he was in trouble.

Glaring at him, Meri's nostrils flared. "My mother was banished from her family because of *him?*" All these years, she had thought her mother chose to leave her relatives behind. It had never occurred to her that her mother had been disowned.

"Yes," he clipped, looking around them as they arrived at their gate. After the pause grew long, he turned to face her squarely, his brow furrowed. "I'm sorry, Meri. I know how painful it must be. I don't really understand what happened between them, and I'm not sure that I want to know any more. I just want to help you out of this mess"— he exhaled loudly—"and be done with it."

The anger plastered across her delicate features, she fumed. "Oh, I see. She loved him, but he didn't give a damn about her!" she accused.

"Now wait a minute!" he tossed back, his own temper flaring. "Obviously that isn't true or we wouldn't be here!"

"Oh? And how do you figure?" she sputtered, her hands flying to her hips in the form of clenched fists.

"He sent me to look out for you"—he shook his head as he spoke—"so it is *implied* that he did care. Otherwise, he wouldn't have bothered even going to her funeral, much less anything else."

"Bullshit," she hissed. "He said he was looking out for

her interests. The book maybe, or their secrets, the tuath or whatever they call themselves. If he cared, he wouldn't have let anything happen to *her*," her voice grew steadily louder, reaching a shout by the end.

"Shhh…" He waved his hands at her. "We're still laying low, remember?"

"Fuck laying low," she only dropped her tone a notch or two, shoving her finger in his face. "Just when I was starting to like you, you do or say something stupid, and I'm back to thinking what an *asshole* you are."

"You were starting to like me?" He grinned, hoping to talk her away from the edge she seemed to be teetering on. "Please, Meri, let's keep it together a little while longer. In a few minutes, we get on the plane, and once we're back in Camden, we can get to the bottom of this. There's no reason for us to be having this fight right now," he implored, noting the stares they had garnered.

He reached for her arm, giving her a squeeze just below the shoulder. Flicking him away, she jerked herself free, her mouth drawn into a tight little pucker. Staring at her, his grin grew even wider at the cuteness of her tantrum. "Ah, Meri," he breathed, longing to pull her close to him.

The idea gave him a jolt, the realization flashing through him like a bolt of lightning. He had known that he liked her, despite telling himself numerous times that he shouldn't. A smart man would steer clear of such a difficult woman, especially since he had sworn off entanglements after the last one had ended so badly. However, discovering that she was not a blood relative, he had found himself elated that he would be free to pursue her if he chose.

"Let's take it easy," he implored. "Please, come and sit with me and at least be civil." He twisted, indicating a row of chairs in the waiting area.

"I don't want to be civil!" she snapped, stepping forward and punching him in the chest. Her eyes instantly wide, her mouth fell open in disbelief, but she held her ground.

Seeing her reaction to her own act of violence, he drew his lips up tight to hide his grin. "Go on then." He spread his hands and indicated his wide target. "Let it out if you need to!"

Snarling, she doubled up her fists and punched him as if he were a bag in a gym, her arms flailing until she couldn't lift them anymore. Sinking into his embrace, she began to cry, sniveling as he held her firmly and caressed her scalp.

"There, there," he soothed. Shushing into her hair, he could feel her sobs wracking her body and tearing at his heart. *Damn*, he muttered to himself. The last thing he had wanted to do was fall in love with her; the best thing he could do now would be to find out who was behind her problems and be done with it quickly, while he could still get away.

His eyes darting around, he could see that more than a few people had watched her little tirade. Feeling the need to explain, he held her firmly and stated to no one in particular, "She just lost her mother."

The crowd of onlookers seemed eager to accept the

explanation, and murmurs of support and condolences passed quickly around the group. Leaving the couple in peace, most moved away or turned their backs, allowing the pair to wait until they were called to board the plane without the interference of strangers.

Again being seated in the front section, with the over-sized seats, Meri flopped down into the one next to the window and covered her face with her hands. Stowing their bag, Rider had fished out his backpack and removed his sketchbook. Placing it in the back of the seat in front of him, he knew spending time on his drawings would calm his nerves and help him deal with the stress that surrounded them.

Sitting back in his seat, he glanced at the woman next to him, noting that she had pulled her hands down and stared out the window with dull, grey eyes. Lifting her hand from the rest between them, he curled her fingers into his, his heart torn by her sniffles.

It was true she had just lost her mother, and that would be as good a reason for her outlandish behavior as any other, but the truth ran much deeper than anything that mundane. His thumb running lightly back and forth across her slender fingers, he replayed the meeting with Eva and what little she had actually told them.

"I think you're right," he said softly. "We'll get a place to stay tonight, and tomorrow we'll check out some of the older cemeteries in the area. See if we can find where your family is buried—especially the ones who made entries in your book."

Blinking at the shadow of the plane as it took off, Meri knew it would be dark before they had landed. "I'm sorry that I hit you," she said in a small voice. "I don't know what came over me."

His grip on her firm, he smiled. "It wasn't a big deal. I'm glad it helped you get a bit of that anger out of your system."

Her mouth twitching, she looked as if she may have more tears to shed before her grief was spent completely. "Do you think that he loved her?" she asked more softly.

"I'm sure that he did." Rider didn't hesitate. "He seemed pretty bothered that their families had kept them apart. He compared the two of them to Romeo and Juliet." He chuckled.

Lifting her head slightly, Merideth swung her gaze to meet his. "Is he as much a romantic as you are?"

Stunned, her companion only stared for a moment, then replied coolly, "Being an artist doesn't make me a romantic."

"Sure it does." She grinned, taken with the need to toy with him. "I know what's in your sketchbook. I saw the last drawing," she teased.

His lips drawn into an *oh* and then sucked inward into an odd pucker, he breathed in shallow pants. "You were snooping through my work?" he asked, refusing to look at the seat in front of him. He still held her hand, his grip growing firmer as he resisted the urge to yank it away from her.

"I wasn't snooping." Her eyes gleamed. "I saw it the other day before all hell broke loose and we left your apartment."

"Ah." He lifted his chin, realizing that meant she had held the knowledge for some hidden reason. If she wanted to hurt him with it, why now? *Here I am being as supportive as I can be, and she wants to rip me to shreds.* Talking about his work could do it, but he wasn't about to let her know that. "It doesn't mean anything," he said aloud and flashed a quick grin. "I draw all sorts of things. That doesn't make them special."

"I thought..." She paused, uncertainty twisting her features. Taking a breath for courage, she insisted, "I thought it meant that you were attracted to me. You know, like, on some deeper level."

"You've either seen too many chick flicks or read too many romance novels." He laughed at her. "I have to admit, you have some nice features, and I enjoyed drawing them, but that's it." His smile etched a strained dimple into his left cheek. "I'm sorry if that hurts you."

"It doesn't hurt me," she denied, pulling her hand free and turning her back on him, hiding her relief. Twisted in her seat in the awkward position, she stared out the window as the darkness stole the clouds from the sky. A few minutes later, she was sound asleep, leaving Rider to wonder if anything she ever told him would make sense.

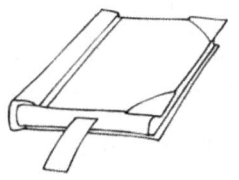

SIXTEEN

Natural Reaction

DOING his best to ignore the woman next to him, Rider opened his sketchbook to a blank page. His hand moving quickly, he placed an outline of a dark figure in the center. Scowling at the image a short time later, he disapproved of her pointed features and sharp nails. Flipping the sheet, he started again, this time choosing a skyline filled with a bright, round moon.

After several minutes, he again felt disturbed by what he had drawn, as leafless trees had crept onto the scene, and a dark foreboding hung over the shadows. Glancing at her, he licked his lips anxiously, then turned back to the original. Adding more details, his fingers moved quickly as sunken cheeks and thin, dry lips emerged.

Using the tip of his pinky, he smudged the wisps of hair that floated around the older woman. Then adding the deep marks once more with the tip of his pencil, he sighed.

"Who is that?" Meri's sharp tone caused him to jump.

Gritting his teeth, he paused, curling the utensil into his palm. "It's no one," he clipped, moving to close the book. Pausing, he studied the older woman. "I don't always use a model. Sometimes, I just make it up as I go."

"She looks evil." The girl stretched, glancing out the portal to her right. "How long before we land?"

"Soon." He flipped the cover shut over his latest creation. "I guess I'm in a foul mood," he surmised aloud. "Normally, my work is very bright, even when I tackle depressing topics, such as the flooded out buildings back in NOLA."

Meri nodded, having to agree. She had been impressed with his talent, but the latest developments in their relationship made it impossible for her to say so. Remaining quiet, she waited for them to land, gripping the armrests hard enough to make her entire fingers white as they descended. Only releasing her grasp once they were on the ground, she leaned into the cushioned seat and sighed with relief. "I'm never flying again."

Chuckling at her observation, he pulled their suitcase out and placed the rest of their belongings inside it. Allowing her to go first, he followed her off the plane and through the tunnel in silence. The air felt cold when they exited the front of the building a short time later. Taking the shuttle to the car lots, they picked up the car they had reserved easily enough, much to Meri's relief.

"Are we staying here tonight or driving straight over to Camden?" she inquired, not sure why he would wait.

"We'll stop at a motel between here and there," he suggested, leaning on his elbow and watching the lights glide by outside. Arriving at the familiar national chain, he could hear her sigh, but she did not complain this time about their simple accommodations. Retrieving their key, he parked the car close to the stairs and opened the trunk. "I'll get the bag if you'll open the door," he stated calmly as he offered her the plastic card.

Clicking her tongue, she accepted it. Her nap on the plane had eased her exhaustion, but she still felt weary at the prospect of another night in what could only be considered a dump by her standards. *Still, it beats sleeping on the ground between the roots of a giant tree.* She sighed to herself.

Leading the way up the flight of metal stairs, she inserted the key and removed it quickly, turning the handle and giving it a push when the green light flickered. As the portal swung wide and she stepped inside, she almost felt overcome by the strong scent of the detergents used to clean the room. "Oh God," she muttered.

Closing the door behind him, Rider could see she had again been offended at his choice. Pulling his backpack out of their uni-bag, he flopped the suitcase open and adjusted the small black stand far enough from the wall that it would stay that way. "Have a shower, Meri," he said in a low tone.

"I'll step outside for half an hour or so and give you some privacy."

When she turned to face him, her breath caught in her chest. His fingers didn't touch her flesh when he reached for her, falling short and dropping back to his side as he turned to exit, but his eyes had said enough. *Shit*. She was in trouble, and she knew it.

After the click of the lock assured her that she had the cramped space to herself, she slowly picked out her clean pair of panties and located the T-shirt he had given her to sleep in a few nights before. A tear trickled down her cheek before she swiped it away almost angrily as she clenched her teeth.

"There will be no time for bawling," she reprimanded herself as she stripped down and closed herself in the smaller compartment containing the toilet and tub. Adjusting the spray as warm as she could take it, she climbed beneath it and leaned against the wall with her forehead pressing against the cool tile.

The warmth of the water streaming across her back relaxed her a bit, and she stood up straight to open the small package of soap. She hated the feeling it left on her delicate skin after it had been rinsed away, not silky and smooth as her body wash at home would have been. "It'll have to do," she murmured.

Clean and resolute to make it through the night without crying, she donned her shirt and slid beneath her covers, fully intending to be asleep before he returned to their quarters and thereby avoiding the situation the man outside presented. On her side and staring at the wall between her and the bathroom, she shuddered. *Will he attack me when he finds out I'm not interested in him?*

The idea that her guardian might turn on her struck fear into her gut, but she had been there before. *Men often don't take rejection well*, she recalled while focusing on her breathing to calm herself further. *Their natural reaction is to attack.* She recalled the few times she had given a man a flat-out refusal and been repaid with harsh words from angry would-be suitors. *God, I don't need this*, she lamented.

One such instance had ended in actual violence and a restraining order. Her fingers lightly tapping the area of her cheekbone for a moment, she recalled the black eye he had given her. "Stupid boy," she muttered into the darkness, fondly recalling her ex-roommate that had been there to save her that day.

It had been the last campus party she had attended while at UCLA, deciding that such alcohol infested gatherings were a ticking time bomb she would do her best to avoid.

Closing her eyes, she focused on the deep inhale and exhale that would lift her to peaceful slumber.

Outside, Rider leaned on the railing and watched the lights of the cars moving on the streets before him, as the motel sat on a slight hill and he had a great view of the city from his vantage point. Standing straight and stretching, he glanced at his watch to discover he had been out there for the better part of an hour—leaning, then pacing, then leaning some more.

Hoping she would be out when he got inside, he opened the door as quietly as he could. Seeing the lump of her beneath her blankets, he felt a flood of relief that he wouldn't have to talk to her again until morning. Pulling his shirt over his head and unbuckling his belt, he ambled towards the shower when the loud singing of his phone brought him to an abrupt halt.

Snatching the device off the small table and flicking open the screen to silence it, he grunted, "Dad."

"Hello, son," his father replied. "I'm in a position to speak now," the older Bradshaw informed him.

"Well, good." Rider kept his voice low and made his way over to his bed. Climbing onto the pliable surface, he leaned against the fake headboard attached to the wall and stretched his legs out before he muttered, "Your friend suggested that we visit Meri's roots. She wants to find where those people in her book are buried."

After a short silence, Thaddeus groaned his agreement. "That would be my guess as well, but I'm not sure how safe it will be."

"Would you happen to know where we should look?" Rider countered, ignoring the warning. They had been in danger since they met. Why should their next step be any different?

"Old Camden Cemetery would be the most likely

place," his father admitted in a somber tone. "Be careful, Rider."

"You knew about the spell book," the younger man challenged in a hiss. "When I read you the translation, you knew Meri's mother was a witch. How deep are you into this, Dad?"

The old man exhaled loudly before he spoke. "I've made some mistakes in my life. Been a part of some things I was too young to realize would haunt me for the rest of my life. Meri's mother is one of those mistakes. I loved Ezamay quite deeply, but our time has passed, and there is no getting it back."

"You didn't answer my question," Rider stated more firmly. His father had a habit of that, he recalled as he considered some of the strange events from his youth that in retrospect indicated that his father may have been a deeper part of the tuath than he cared to admit. "Are you a witch?"

"I have certain amounts of knowledge," his raspy voice carried over the line. "Please, son. Don't judge an old man for the life he was born to live. Take care of Merideth. See to it that she discovers what she must."

Rider's heart skipped a beat at his father's final words, finding them too similar to their benefactor in NOLA to ignore. Glancing at the device to see that the call had in fact ended, he groaned. "Silly old codger. As if I would back out now." He scoffed, glancing over at the sleeping form to his left. With only the light on in the bathroom, the room had been dimly lit, but he could make out her form as her steady breathing caused the lump of her to rise and fall in an even rhythm.

Laying his phone on the nightstand, he resumed his quest for a shower before turning in. His mind filled with images of her expressive features, he allowed the thoughts to churn and grow as he bathed; her smiles might have been few and fleeting, but the joy they gave him was unmistakable. *Damn it.* He struck the wall with the side of his fist, causing a loud thump.

How many days does it take to fall in love?

Apparently not many, he mentally argued with himself, taking on both sides of the conversation. *I'm so fucked.*

Cutting off the spray and grabbing a fresh towel, he swiped it over his body before he applied it vigorously to his hair. Slipping into his boxer briefs, his groin ached. She had promised him friend sex, but he doubted that he would ever collect, even if she were willing. Doing so would be his downfall, there wasn't an ounce of doubt in his mind about it.

SEVENTEEN

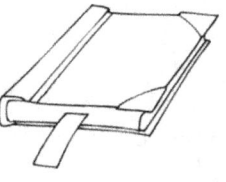

Déjà vu

_____

TENSION FILLED the room as the couple took turns using the toilet and dressing for their trip to the graveyard. After brushing her teeth and applying only a small amount of makeup, Meri inspected herself in the mirror while considering whether to put her hair up or allow it to hang free. Catching Rider's covert glances, her features twisted into an annoyed scowl.

"I can't wait for this to be over," she announced loudly.

"Yeah, that makes two of us," he agreed, turning his back as he gathered his things and shoved them into their suitcase.

"I doubt that," she spat, her forehead creased with deep lines. Her night of brooding in fear had brought out her stubborn, rebellious streak, and she felt the undeniable urge to put him in his place.

His unshaven chin lifting slowly, he blinked at her.

Rubbing the thick stubble anxiously, he commented, "If you have something to say, you might as well get on with it. I'm not afraid of you, Meri."

"Afraid of me," she gasped. "I didn't say you were afraid!"

"No, you haven't said much of anything, to be exact. You are a prudish woman destined to live the life of an old spinster," he concluded and continued his packing.

I knew it! She smirked to herself. *He knows I'm not going to tumble into his arms, so he'll turn on me. Asshole.* Aloud she clipped pointedly, "I guess the honeymoon is over?"

Cutting his eyes over at her, he held his calm demeanor. "I guess that it is. I guess saying that I've grown quite fond of you would be a moot point."

Meri glared at him, her shocked expression plain to see. *He's trying to trick me and wear down my defenses*, she mused. "Flattery will get you nowhere, sir."

His laugh loud and unexpected, she jumped at his reply. "Flattery? Is that what you think this is?" He stepped towards her, and she backed against the counter, pressing it hard against her rear. Her chin quivered as his hand found her cheek, his palm sliding along her jaw before his finger traced her pout-perfect lips.

"Oh, Meri," he breathed. "I couldn't sleep last night. I just lay there thinking about you."

"Stop it," she hissed, slapping at his hand, which he refused to remove. "I said stop!" her voice cracked as her anger gave way to terror. She had come close to being raped before after denying a man what he wanted, and the memory of it sent her pounding heart into fits of chaos.

Standing straighter, he scowled down at her. "What's wrong with you? I just want to talk. Can't we talk for a minute?" He stared into her clouded brown orbs, his gut wrenching at the fear he could clearly read within them. "Meri, I'm not going to hurt you. I would *never* hurt you."

"Right. Because you're sworn to protect me," she whispered.

"No, not for that." He shook his head slowly. "Because I like you. I really...like you. It's been a long time since I could say that to a woman, and quite frankly, I never thought that I would ever again. But I have to. I have to tell you while I still can because I'm not sure how all this is going to work out."

"Oh really," her condescending tone cut like a knife. "Long enough to get me into bed, I presume. I told you I've changed my mind. I don't want to sleep with you."

"I'm not talking about sex, love," he breathed, his face moving slowly closer to hers as if he intended to kiss her. "You've done something to me. Awakened something I thought I had managed to bury so deep no one could reach it."

"You're pathetic." She gave him a shove, pushing her way past him. "Do you really think I'm ignorant enough to fall for a line like that? Next, you'll be talking about our future and how great we would be together." She marched towards the door before spinning to face him. "I have news for you, mister." She pointed an accusing finger. "We are nothing alike, and getting into a relationship with you would be about the stupidest thing I could ever do."

The night before she had rationalized that she needed to save her rejection until their situation had been resolved. *Damn him for pushing this*, she seethed before she blasted him with the truth. "I know where I'm going in my life, and it's not your way. You're a lost child, living in some dream world, with no ambition, with no future, painting your silly little pictures and drawing your crumbling buildings. Let's get this done so I can get back to my life, which could never include you."

When he only glowered at her, she backed towards the exit slowly, expecting him to leap at her at any moment. The muscle in his jaw tightened, but he made no such move, and a full minute passed as they stared each other down.

"Fine," he finally stated tersely. "I said what I needed to say." Slapping the bag shut, he zipped it and cast his eyes hurriedly around the room. "Do we have everything?"

Her mouth hung open, uncharacteristically in shock at his reaction. "Yes," she breathed, opening the door and stepping out onto the balcony to find a thin layer of frost covered everything. Her heart calming into a quick patter, she couldn't believe she had spoken to him in such a manner or that he had accepted the hurtful words so calmly. *Good. Maybe that will be the end of that rubbish*, she hoped as she descended the stairs and headed for their car.

STOPPING FOR BREAKFAST, the silence hung around them like a shroud. Taking their seats at a table in a small diner, Meri accepted the chair that he held for her out of polite custom. Sitting beside her, Rider could feel the chill emanating from her rigid form, but he didn't dare voice his apology or ask for hers. They had work to be done, in a manner of speaking, and when this was over, he would gladly go back to his solitary existence. *My little paintings, ha!*

Watching her as she ate with her perfectly sized bites and her pretty mouth crinkling as she chewed, he despised the ache in his chest. The déjà vu he felt at being hurt by another woman tore at him. He had protected himself well since he had tossed his ex out of his life, the memory of her betrayal a firm reminder of why he was better off alone. He didn't need the woman next to him, and the fact that he wanted her only served to fuel his resignation that they were better off apart, despite what the beat of his heart might be telling him.

Leaving the small diner, Meri finally broke the silence with a pointed question. "Where are we going?"

"My father called last night. I told him we needed to find where your ancestors were buried, and he suggested the Old Camden Cemetery. I'm not sure if he's right, but it's worth a shot."

"Oh," she breathed, unaware that he actually had a plan.

Turning to face her window, she watched the buildings pass by, trying to force her mind into the familiar and considering what they might look like on the inside. Seeing him peek at his phone from the corner of her eye, she snapped, "Are you texting and driving?"

"No." He huffed. "I'm using Google Maps to get us there more efficiently."

"Give me that." She snatched the device from his hand. "Make a left here." Staring at the screen, she took over the navigation. "Were you afraid to ask for directions?" she observed with a slight giggle.

"Obviously not." He indicated the cell.

"Then why didn't you ask me to help?"

"I figured you were mad."

"Mad or not, I still would have helped. It's on the right up here, so turn on this street coming up."

Making the turn onto the narrow path, they slowed and watched out the left side of the car. Spying a one-way sign pointing the opposite direction, he spat, "Shit. You had me turn at the wrong place!"

"No, I didn't," she countered, holding out the screen. "It said to turn right!" Gripping the armrest as he performed a U-turn using the narrow median, she stared out her window at the graves next to the fence. A strange feeling of mild panic tightened her chest, and she exhaled heavily in an effort to remove it.

Turning right and pulling down the other side of the gated area, he pointed. "There's the entrance."

"No, don't!" she called loudly, clamping onto his arm at the same time. "Park on the street. Please don't pull in there!"

Flicking his eyes over at her a few times as he guided the vehicle to the curb, he lowered his voice. "What's the matter? We're not even sure this is the place."

"This is the place," she breathed, releasing him and opening the door to climb out. Walking a few paces, her fingers slid between the links in the metal fence, and she pressed her face against it so she could stare through one of the squares.

"How do you know?" he asked, instinctively placing his right hand on the small of her back while the left held her mother's tome firmly against his broad chest.

"I need my jacket," she announced as she slipped from his grasp and turned back to the car to retrieve his leather coat from the back seat. Dropping it over her shoulders, she felt a small twinge of guilt at the harsh words she had sprayed upon him earlier that morning. He had been nothing but good to her; he didn't deserve to be belittled.

Rejoining him, she reached for the book and pulled it flat against her bosom. The pair ambled towards the wide opening that served as the driveway, but judging from the amount of foliage covering the area, it received little use. "How do you know this is the place?" he tried again, anxious at her changed demeanor.

"A feeling." She flittered a brief smile. Walking between the metal poles, their slow amble came to a full stop as she cast her eyes across the barren trees and dead grass. Many of the headstones sat at odd angles or lay toppled over onto the ground. "This place is very old," she hissed. Moving again, she headed for a tall marker close to the center.

"Meri, wait." He reached for her arm. Finding her hand, he curled her fingers between his. "Tell me what's going on."

"I don't know." She glanced up at him, allowing him to hold her. "I feel connected to this place—as if I can't breathe, and my flesh tingles." Walking a few more yards, she pulled him along before making an abrupt turn and guiding him through a patch of stones. "They're over here," she said more confidently.

Allowing her to take the lead, Rider watched around them anxiously. The place deserted, he would easily see anyone who tried to approach. However, being out in the open also meant that anyone in the apartments that surrounded the graveyard could watch them, unseen. He didn't like the idea and dropped her hand when she stopped to continue his surveillance by making a slow circle around her.

Opening the diary, Merideth caught the feather that had fallen out of the binding before it could float away on the slight breeze. Toying with it between her slender fingers, she turned the pages slowly, comparing the names and dates to those on the stones before her. "Here's one," she exclaimed, using the white plume to indicate the name.

"This was written about ten years before she died," she stated excitedly at the discovery. "We really found them!"

His unease growing with every minute that passed, Rider stepped up beside her to make the comparison for himself. "Ok, so now what?" he asked absently.

Her eyes dancing, Meri turned to face him. "Where's the translation for my mother's spell?"

"It's folded inside the back cover. Why? You're not going to read it, are you?"

"Of course I am." She beamed. Locating the pages, she opened them with trembling digits.

"Do you think that's the smart thing to do?" he demanded. "My father freaked out when he heard what was on that page."

"I don't care. My mother wrote it. She must have had a purpose, having given the book to me, and I feel like that's the logical thing to do. I have found the resting place of my ancestors, and I need to read my mother's spell," she informed him matter-of-factly.

Moving to stand beside her, Rider waited. Listening to her voice read aloud for the second time since he met her, he could feel the cool breeze on his face as it lifted and teased her hair. Catching the strands and smoothing them out of her face, he sighed deeply, catching the phrase: *The truth of the past is undeniable, the beauty of the present is unequivocal, and the wisdom of the future is unconventional.*

"That was a strange thing to say," he interrupted her.

"Please, let me finish." She smiled at him briefly before continuing, sending his heart racing.

How does she do that to me? he demanded silently to himself. *Unconventional...* He turned the word over in his mind. *Does that mean that the future is not what we expect it to be?* Shaking off the query, he stepped away and left her to her recitation, still uncertain what she hoped to accomplish by it. Glancing around at the collection of graves, he froze at the sight of someone on the other side of the lot.

"Meri!" he gasped. "There's a woman over there!" He pointed at the slight frame wrapped in a plain, black, knee-length coat.

Lifting her gaze from her small sheaf of papers, Meri's voice cracked, "Oh my God. It's my mother!" Without hesitating, she took off at a full run, the heavy leather jacket and her mother's text weighing her down. Her eyes fixed on the woman who appeared to be studying another of the headstones, she missed a step and fell over a toppled marker, twisting her ankle.

Only half a step behind, Rider dropped to his knees beside her. "Are you ok?"

"No. I've injured myself," she stated between sobs. Pulling at her pant leg, she tried to look at the injured joint, while hoping it wasn't broken. Then, remembering the woman, she turned back in her direction, ready to call out to her. "Where'd she go?"

Following her gaze for a moment before returning his attention to the injured appendage, he growled, "Who knows. She seems to have disappeared. Maybe we imagined her."

"We *both* imagined her?" Meri clipped angrily, adding special emphasis to the word *both*. "You know that's impossible. One of us might have been hallucinating but not both of us. Not the same thing."

Nodding, he didn't want to argue. Picking up the book in one hand, he stood and held out the other to her. "Let's see if you can stand."

Getting to her feet with a good degree of assistance, tears streaked her face. "It hurts," she sobbed. Putting more weight on it, she hissed, "I think I can make it to the car, but beyond that, I won't be much good." Her eyes flicking around them, she sighed. "I know it was her."

"Well, we can't prove that. All we can say is that her being there and then disappearing was damn strange," he concluded, offering her his arm. "Lean on me if you need to, and we'll go back to the car. Did you finish reading your spell to your relatives?" he half joked with her.

"Yes, I read it all," she said through gritted teeth. "I read hers, too—the woman buried there, that is. I have no idea what it meant since it was in Gaelic, but I think she will understand my sentiment."

"Forget about it," he instructed. "We came as directed. I'll call my dad once we are back in the car and see if he has any ideas as far as what we should do next."

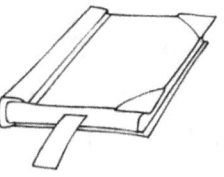

EIGHTEEN

Inverted

HOLDING Meri up as she hobbled along, Rider muttered to himself. A strong, frigid wind had kicked up as soon as they started moving, and just as they reached the wide gate, cold rain splatted his face with huge drops of moisture. Only glancing up at the thick mass of grey clouds above them, he stopped her and shoved her mother's book inside the leather jacket that Meri wore.

"Hang on," he commanded, sweeping her off her feet and making wide strides to their waiting rental. Struggling to open the door without putting her down, he managed to grasp the handle. As soon as her toes touched the earth, she pivoted and dropped into the seat, pelted by the onslaught as the heavens opened up.

Drenched, Rider scurried around the back end of the car, then paused with his hand on his own handle. "What the hell?" he mumbled, staring as two figures walked along the median next to the fence of the graveyard. They were still on the far side of the entrance, but it wouldn't take them long to reach the couple, a realization that plunged his scattered thoughts into dark panic.

Jerking open his door, he climbed in and immediately started the car. Swinging it around before even bothering with his seatbelt, Meri leaned one way and then the other.

Fighting to hold on, she demanded, "What's the matter with you? Is a twisted ankle not injury enough?"

Grasping the rear-view mirror, he adjusted it a bit to the side so he could see that the couple that had been approaching had stopped. Losing them as the back window fogged over, he cursed and searched for the button that would turn on the rear defroster. "Someone was coming," he informed her in a hoarse whisper. "I think from those apartments on that side. Who knows how long they had been watching us."

Leaning to look between the seats, Meri couldn't see anything behind them in the downpour. "What makes you think they were after us?" she demanded angrily.

"Why wouldn't they be?" he snapped, wiping at his wet hair to smooth it back into place. "Everywhere we have gone, everything we have done has led to someone being after us."

"I want to go home," she replied. "This is too ludicrous to even imagine."

"Do you still think she was your mother?" he countered while digging for his phone.

"Absolutely."

"Then we should go and pay your father a visit instead," he urged, flicking open the screen.

"My father," she whined, adjusting her foot as waves of angry pain shot up her leg. "Rider, I'm sorry. I may have to have a doctor."

Pausing before placing his call, he glanced at her to note her pale, almost ghostly complexion. Handing her the device, he commanded, "Locate a hospital, and we'll get it x-rayed. I'll call Dad after we get there."

Accepting the role of navigator once more, she located the nearest facility and gave him directions through gritted teeth. "It didn't hurt this bad a while ago," she admitted between pants.

"Of course not," he soothed, reaching to pat her knee gently. "The rush of adrenaline covers it, but once that wears off, you get the full effect of the damage. Don't worry. We'll get you patched up."

The warmth of his hand felt comforting through her damp jeans, and she fought the tears that threatened to escape by biting her lip. Watching the rain-soaked street zooming past, she leaned her head back and closed her eyes. "Do you think my father has something to do with all of this?"

"He must," Rider insisted. "He arranged your mom's funeral. If she isn't really dead, then he would know about it and why all of this is happening." Pulling into the drive-up area of the emergency room, he pointed. "Hang on, and I'll get a wheelchair from over there."

Not moving, Meri waited for his return, then placed her feet gingerly on the ground when he opened the door. Standing, she limped in a small circle and took the seat. "Thank you."

"You're welcome." He smiled, pushing her inside. Leaving her at the check-in, he returned to the car and parked it in the garage across the street. Opening his phone once more as he arrived back at the entrance, he made the call to his father anxiously. Not waiting for pleasantries, he dove right in as soon as the man answered. "What the hell is going on?" he bit angrily.

"Well, hello," Thaddeus retorted.

"Stow it," Rider shot back. "You sent me to protect this girl because her mother had been murdered, only her mother isn't dead!" he announced confidently.

Silence met his accusation for a long moment before his father spoke in a calm voice. "What makes you think she isn't?"

"We saw her! At that cemetery you sent us to. And then, some creepy guys showed up just as we were getting in the car!"

"What did they say to you?" Thad asked anxiously.

"Nothing. We got the hell out of there before they got to us. Meri hurt herself—fell in a hole while running to catch her mother. We're getting her ankle x-rayed, and we didn't wait around to see what they wanted."

"Ezamay," Thad hissed, barely above a whisper. "Did they get her?"

"No. She disappeared before they showed up," Rider said with a loud sigh. "Dad, I wish you could just be honest with me. What the hell is going on?"

"In time, son," his father cajoled. "Right now, take care of Meri. I'll arrange a meeting place, and we'll get to the bottom of this."

"Sure, Dad." Rider winced. He had never had any reason to doubt his father's word, but this latest turn of events made his blind faith in the older man suddenly feel quite foolish. "You do that." He ended the call and pulled the pack of cigarettes out of his pocket. He had used them as a ruse to spend time outside their hotel rooms and give Meri some space, but at the moment, he intended to enjoy a real smoke and hoped that it would calm his raw nerves.

Inside the waiting area, Merideth sat in her wheelchair with her foot elevated. Glaring at the glass windows that made up the exterior wall and entrance, she could see Rider talking on the phone while pacing back and forth in front of the glass. His demeanor put her on edge, and she wondered if it was a mistake to trust him. Her entire life had been inverted and teetering on the edge of chaos since she met him, and although she felt like he wanted to help her, she couldn't be sure that he actually was.

"Merideth Monroe," a male voice called from the double doors leading to the back.

"Here." She waved at him, irritated that her companion remained outside.

Striding over to her, the tall, dark-haired young man smiled down at her. "Don't worry, miss. I'll push you back." Guiding the chair expertly, they left the waiting area and moved to a treatment room. Pushing her into the small cubical, he nodded. "The doctor will be here in a moment to give it a look, but I'm sure you'll be headed to x-ray," he informed her after removing her shoe and rolling her pant leg up a few times.

Laying a gown on the bed, he requested, "Pull off your pants and put the gown on over your shirt, unless you'd rather undress completely."

Staring at him with a half-open jaw, Meri wasn't sure how to take the comment. Choosing to ignore it, she agreed, "Thanks."

Alone a moment later, she managed to get to her feet. Forced to remove the jacket, she tossed it onto the only chair in the cramped space. Able to slide her pants down to her knees while balancing on her good leg, she pulled the gown on backwards, with the opening in the back, and then sat again to remove the jeans. Giving them a quick fold, they landed on top of the jacket. Adjusting the thin cloth over her lap, she shivered. She wished they had given her an actual blanket and considered whether she could use the coat to cover her legs.

"Meri!" Rider announced himself as he adjusted the curtain back into place. Looking down at her pitiful appearance, his scowl deepened. Sitting on the edge of the chair and leaning towards her, he whispered, "We have to talk."

"I'm sure we do," she agreed with a sniff, "but can you get me a blanket first? I'm freezing!"

"Sure, baby," he agreed obediently, leaving her long enough to visit the nurse's station and retrieve one. Spreading it over her when he returned, he noticed her twisted expression anxiously. "Here you go," he soothed, wishing he could ease her pain.

"I'm fine," she snapped. "Don't call me *baby*. I'm not your girl, and I won't ever be your girl."

"That's what you're upset about?" He stared at her incredulously. "It's just a word, Meri. I didn't mean anything by it!"

"Sure." She raised her chin and hissed, "What did your father say?"

"He's going to arrange a meeting place for us." He reclaimed the seat and again leaned towards her to keep his voice low. "He didn't deny that your mother is alive, either. He sounded concerned that those two goons I saw might have gotten her."

Closing her eyes slowly, the girl's blood boiled. "This is your fault," she said, her voice almost inaudible.

"My fault?" He sat up straight and stabbed himself in the chest with a stiff finger. "How is it my fault?"

"It makes sense." She remained still while she accused him of treachery. "You and your father planned this some-how. You've known all along that she wasn't dead, leading me around on this crazy escapade. Why? What are you getting out of this?" Her blue orbs popped open and glared at him.

Rider's Adam's apple bobbed up and down as he swallowed hard a few times. "Meri, I swear to you. I had no idea that she wasn't in that casket. I've done everything I can to protect you and keep you safe, and I certainly am not part of whatever is going on."

In that instant, a thought occurred to him, and he gasped. "Your mother is part of this. She set it up. She had to."

"Do not accuse my mother of anything!" Meri demanded, tightening her arms across her chest.

"Meri, see reason. It was her book and her spell. Her accident and her funeral. Your mother is at the center of this. I'm sure of it."

"Hello!" a loud, friendly voice interrupted their conversation as the doctor pulled back the curtain and entered her cubical. Lifting the blanket while introducing himself, the doctor gave no indication that he had heard or cared about the matter the two had been discussing.

Watching and listening as his companion made an excuse as to how her condition had occurred, Rider's thoughts churned. A deep ache had settled in his chest at the realization that her mother was involved in the mess that they found themselves in. He hated that Meri refused to see it and realized that they were probably in more danger now than they had ever been in before.

NINETEEN

Notorious

FOUR HOURS LATER, Rider pulled their rental car up at the exit to retrieve the girl. She looked adorable in the new pink sweatsuit he had purchased for her in the gift shop. *No way her jeans were going to fit over that boot they put on her leg*, he mused.

Climbing out, he made his way around to help her inside and then placed the plastic bag containing her original wardrobe into the back seat with the rest of their belongings. "I'm glad it's not broken," he announced as he snapped his seatbelt into place and helped her with hers.

"Where are we going?" she asked meekly, the pain meds she had been given bringing her attitude down considerably.

"My father texted me an address about an hour ago," he replied as he made a right turn and pointed them in the proper direction while hitting the wipers to combat the drizzle that remained after the morning's rain. "Relax, and we'll be there in a bit." He didn't want to delve back into the subject they had been discussing before the doctor's arrival and hoped Meri would continue to let it lie.

"I'm sorry, Rider," she said quietly.

Damn. She's going to bring it up, he realized in silence. When she didn't go on, he acknowledged her efforts aloud. "Ok. Let's talk about it, then."

"I think you could be right. My mother would have to have been an active participant. All of them would be complicit. They would have to be for everything to fall into place as it did," she lamented.

Reaching for her leg, Rider gave her knee a squeeze. "Don't worry. I've got your back. And don't read anything into that. We're friends in the least, and you can count on me to stand up for you."

A tear trickled down her cheek, and she swiped it away. Pressing her lips together tightly for a moment, she pushed on. "I feel like we're some notorious outlaws, like Bonnie and Clyde. Everyone is looking for us, and we have nowhere to hide."

Rider chuckled at the analogy. "Are you saying we should run away rather than meet with them?"

"What good would it do? We have to face them. We can't escape, and in the end, we have to know why she did this to me—why they did this to us." She fought the urge to take his hand and fold it between hers. She honestly still considered him to be a part of *they*, and there would be no one she could trust or turn to. "Just take me to them, and let's get this over with."

Closing her eyes, Meri rested until the car came to a stop and Rider killed the engine. Sitting up and waiting for him to help her out, she stared up at the large house, guessing it to be at least a hundred years old, if not more. Accepting his hand, she stood shakily beside him. Noting he had brushed his hair and it once again lay smooth against his head and pulled back into its customary ponytail, she smiled in spite of her distrust of him. "Thank you."

"Don't mention it," he replied, placing his arm around her as he walked her up the long path. Ahead of them, he admired the veranda that ran along the front and disappeared around the left hand side of the house. Huge windows stared back at him, with several bay windows sticking out the front of the three-story structure. "Damn, this place is ancient," he mused.

"Yes," Meri agreed, their kindred spirit and understanding of architecture and design drawing her to him for a moment. "Can you imagine what the two of us could do with this place?"

Chuckling, he agreed, "It has a lot of potential," as if they were newlyweds out searching for their first home.

Mounting the stairs, the couple made it to the door just as it opened before them. A young woman in a plain black dress held it for them and gestured for them to enter. Moving past her in unison, they removed their coats and allowed her to take them. Her eyes flicking to Rider's pack, he shook his head and returned it to his shoulder. Pointing to the parlor to the left, she indicated for them to enter without so much as a word.

The air felt cold as they stepped inside, and Rider instinctively pulled his shivering charge against him. His eyes dark, he glared at each figure standing or sitting about the room. "Well, fancy meeting all of you here," he finally taunted.

Meri said nothing, her heart beating wildly inside her chest. To their left, a pair of gentlemen stood next to the front window. Dressed in dark suits, beards of deep-red hair covered their faces, and crinkled flesh surrounded their eyes. Diverting her gaze, she could see two women seated on the couch before the two men, and to their left sat an older woman with shining white hair in a large flower-print chair.

Following the circle of the room, a fireplace filled with a roaring blaze stood in the center of the far wall, its mantle and both sides covered in a collage of black-and-white pictures featuring a multitude of people whom she did not recognize. Her eyes making it to the right side of the gathering, Thaddeus stood to the right of the hearth, and her mother sat on the sofa next to him, where his hand rested on her shoulder. A woman shared the seat with Ezamay, and behind them stood an older woman and man, also unknown to her.

"Who are you people?" Meri demanded when she had finished inspecting them. Her jaw quivered, and she clenched her teeth, unwilling to let them see how moved she felt at having the older Monroe's deceit confirmed.

"Meri," her mother called softly. "Please, come and sit down," she said as she patted the cushion next to her.

Tightening his grip, Rider prevented her from moving despite her injured state. "We'll stand, thanks."

"This is nonsense," one of the two older men to the left interjected. "We demand a ruling in this matter, Minerva!" he addressed the woman in the chair.

"In time, Aenjus," the elderly woman soothed in a raspy voice. Staring at Meri, she grated, "We require the tome."

A tear forming in her eye, the girl shook her head slowly, shrugging as she professed, "I don't have it."

"It's in here," Rider interrupted, dropping his pack off of his shoulder as he released her.

Glaring at him, Meri hissed, "You brought it with us?"

Offering her an upturned palm, his expression begged forgiveness. "Like we had anywhere to hide it. Be reasonable."

Stepping past them, Thad left the room as his son unzipped the tattered bag, returning a moment later with a pair of straight-backed chairs from the dining room. "Here," he commanded, placing them behind their guests. "Sit down and give that foot a rest."

Smearing her drops of sadness with the back of her hand, Meri obeyed, taking the seat as Rider placed her mother's book on the table before her, then sat in his own chair. Opening it to the spell she had read at the graveyard, the bright white feather lay sandwiched between the pages.

"Oh," Ezamay gasped at the sight of the plume.

Her fingers shaking, Meri caressed the stiff spine and explained, "It fell out of the binding. But you already knew it was there, didn't you?" she accused, cutting her eyes up at her mother.

"Yes." A tear spilled over from the older woman's blue orbs. "I hid it there. I didn't think you would discover it."

Lifting the feather, Merideth touched it gently to her lips, the warm air brushing its tendrils and causing them to flutter. "You put a spell on it. Some kind of charm to make me fall in love with Rider."

Her mother's eyes grew wide as an audible gasp escaped from the two women who sat on the couch to her left, facing her. "I did no such thing," she denied. "It was a binding—meant to repair the damage between our families. It is time that the old feud is put to rest."

"Agreed," Minerva spoke sternly.

"But that is not her tome to give," Aenjus accused. "She has been disowned by her clan!"

"It is mine to give!" the woman seated on the couch with Ezamay spoke for the first time. "I am the last remaining female of the Quinn, and I have passed my right to my sister."

Staring at her in disbelief, Merideth's voice quavered, "You're my aunt?"

"I am, child," the woman confirmed. "I am Elizabeth. I have no daughters, and you are the last of our line."

Her face growing red, Meri could feel the rage swelling inside her. "My mother said the same thing when she gave the book to me. What exactly is it that you have been up to?" she demanded, her eyes darting between them.

"Disobedience and treachery," Aenjus fumed. "Your line is gone. You have no rights here, child of an outcast. Leave the book and be gone!"

Swinging her glare to the man who had spoken to her, she blinked at him for a moment before dropping her gaze to the women seated on the sofa before him. "And you are?"

"These are my aunts," Rider informed her, cocking his head towards them. "Brigit and Bronagh. They are my mother's sisters."

Her features growing twisted, Merideth sat up straight in the chair as she searched face after face. "Would someone please tell me what the hell is going on here?" Her voice cracked as she begged, "I'm so tired, and I just want the truth." Narrowing her eyes into slits, they bore into her mother. "Why did you fake your own death? How could you do this to me?"

Standing abruptly, her mother moved forward and pushed the tome to the side. Taking a seat on the coffee table, she took the girl's hands and clasped them within hers. "I did not fake my death, sweetheart. The accident was real, and it is only by a miracle that I sit before you."

Meri's shoulders shook as she sobbed. "How can I believe that?"

"Meri, darling, please listen to me," her mother tried to explain.

"No," Aenjus interrupted once more. "We have rules, laws that must be followed. Minerva, I'm warning you—"

"Sit down, brother," Brigit commanded. "It is up to the women to decide this matter." Glaring at him over her right shoulder, the older woman waited until he had taken a seat in a stuffed chair in the corner before she addressed the girl before her. "We have an accord. The feud that has raged between our families has cursed us. While other clans have thrived, our two have dwindled from a gushing spring of life and prosperity to a dying trickle on the brink of extinction. We agree that binding the rift is the only way to end our downward spiral."

"I knew it!" Meri gasped, her eyes darting quickly around the ring of women. "You do intend to force me into a relationship with him. Well, it won't work! I'm onto your magic, your alluring sorcery!"

Giving her a squeeze, Ezamay chided, "That's not what a binding is for, love. It merely has awakened your under- standing of your line, of your identity. It has given you the knowledge to release us all from centuries of dark sadness. Any love you feel for this man is of your own heart's creation."

Her chest tight, Merideth didn't dare look at Rider. Biting her lip, she pouted for a moment before she asked more softly, "If you were really dead, then how is it that you are now alive?"

"That bit of magic relied on you." Her mother smiled deviously. "I couldn't simply tell you all of this. I had tried, several times, and each one of them you pushed me away. I had to show you who you are, what you are capable of doing. You are the future of our clan—the last female in the line of the Quinn."

"Stop saying that." Meri jerked her hands free. "Get away from me!"

Blinking rapidly, Ezamay complied by moving back to her cushion on the couch. Once she had been reseated, she drew a deep breath and tried again. "Meri, I know this is difficult for you. I know you had your dreams, and they will still be yours. We will not force you to take your place as the matriarch of our family." She cast a furtive glance at her sibling. "But we do ask that you release the Bradshaws from the curse."

A look of horror washing across her face, the bright pink of her outfit seemed at odds with her doleful expression as Meri whined, "And how exactly am I going to do that?"

"Turn the pages, Meri," Minerva commanded.

"And? Half of this dammed thing is in Gaelic. How am I supposed to know which spell to use?" she bit angrily.

"Listen to your heart, child," the mediator instructed.

Seeing the man who remained standing to her left fidget, Merideth cast a few rapid glances in his direction before she persisted. "It was you guys. You're the ones who broke into my mother's office and trashed my apartment. You were looking for the book."

"She had no right to give it to you," Aenjus spoke from his seat, not daring to stand. "We only wanted to take it from you and to prevent you from discovering the truth."

Her fingers trembling, Meri slowly turned the pages with her left hand, her right still fondling the feather and swiping it gently across her lips. A warm feeling in the pit of her gut caused her to flush. "I'm a witch, aren't I," she breathed.

When no one responded, she lifted her chin. "It's ok. You don't have to tell me. I can feel it." She smiled slightly. Stopping at a page not far from the beginning, she felt butterflies dancing in her chest. "This is it," she breathed. Her voice low, she read the spell as she had the one in the graveyard.

"Meri, I'm not sure this is a good idea," Rider stated, his voice filled with mild alarm.

"Be quiet," Bronagh commanded.

His eyes lifting to glare at her, Rider could see dark clouds hanging low through the window over her shoulder. "Meri, I said I don't think this is a good idea," he stated more forcefully. Reaching out to grab his companion's arm, a jolt of electricity greeted him, and he yanked his hand away. "Oww! Son of a bitch!"

Her chant unbroken, Merideth continued to read, a bolt of lightning flashing outside, followed by an instant boom that plunged the room into near darkness. The dancing light from the fire casting long shadows across the wall, Meri lifted the bottom edge of the book to catch the rays and complete the spell.

"Merideth, I said stop!" Rider howled, finding his feet and reaching for her again. This time, when their flesh met, a loud crack, like the sound of a whip, tore through the air, knocking him down an instant before a gust of wind slammed against the house, extinguishing the fire and plunging the group into a blackness impossible to penetrate.

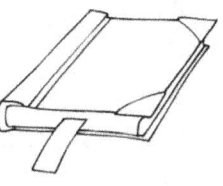

TWENTY

Golden Age

RIDER COULD HEAR MUFFLED voices moving around him. Fighting the weight of his eyelids, he struggled to force them open. Exhaling loudly, he rested for a moment and then tried again. Managing a pair of narrow slits, he could see bright red and blue lights flashing off the side of what remained of the house.

Getting his bearings, he realized after a few minutes that he lay on a gurney out in the yard. An ambulance began to wail as it pulled away, and he watched it roll past the other emergency vehicles before it exited the drive. His throat dry, he coughed a few times before he croaked, "What the hell is going on?"

"Hey there." A pretty, young brunette smiled down at him, adjusting the mask over his face. "Just breathe, big guy. Your friends are all safe. We're getting you all transported as quickly as we can."

Blinking up at her, Rider processed the information. *Something happened.* "Was it a fire?" he gasped.

"No. A small twister cut through the property. Demolished half the house and a couple of the neighbors' as well before it dissipated."

"That's a shame," he muttered, exhaustion getting the better of him and forcing his mind back into oblivion.

Sometime later, he again found consciousness, this time aware of the dim lights overhead. Blinking at the square tiles of the ceiling, his hand found his face, only this time, only his scraggly beard could be found.

"Well hello, son," his father's voice cut through the silence.

"Dad?" Rider whispered. "Why am I in a hospital?" he asked before he recalled the conversation with the medic.

Towering over him, the senior Bradshaw ruffled his hair as if he were still a boy. "Relax, son. We're all safe. A tornado is to blame for the abrupt end to our party."

"Sure. Is that what you called it?"

"That's what the emergency response team called it," Thad informed him. "What it really was…is hard to say."

"Where's Meri?"

"Down the hall, with her mother. I'll let her know you're awake if you can stand a visit." Thaddeus turned towards the door.

"Did she free your curse or whatever the hell this was all about?" Rider demanded, recalling more details about their evening.

"Yes, she did. She did a right fine job," his father muttered, allowing the door to close behind him.

His fingers searching the buttons on the side of the bed, Rider found the one that would raise his head and pushed it firmly. Adjusting the inclined position, he lifted his blanket to discover he wore a thin hospital gown and nothing else. Not seeing any obvious wounds, he scowled. "Where the hell are my clothes?"

"In the cupboard," Meri replied with a grin as she entered and closed the entrance behind her. "You took quite a blow to the head, sir." Taking the stool from the corner, she pushed it up to the side of the bed and sat gingerly upon it with her foot extended out beside her. Her fingers pushing his hair aside lightly, she said more softly, "You're lucky."

"Lucky." He chortled. "Lucky to be alive, is that it?"

"Yes, partly." She pursed her lips. "I hadn't realized how much I had grown to care about you until I had to choose. I could ride in the ambulance with my mother or wait and ride in the next one with you."

"I guess your mom won," he observed with a flick of his wrist that exposed his open palm to her. "Or am I wrong?"

"You're not wrong." She sighed, her eyes falling to stare at her lap as she toyed with her fingers. "I rode with my mother. I didn't think I would ever be able to live with myself if she died a second time and I wasn't with her."

"So how is she?"

"She's stable. She was close to the window, and when it blew in, she took a fair amount of glass to the face and upper body." Meri shivered as she gave her description. "They're going to have a plastic surgeon visit her tomorrow to see about repairing some of the damage."

"Wow," Rider breathed, "I'm sorry to hear that. Are you ok?"

"Oh, I'm fine." She smiled, giddy for a brief moment. "My injured foot has been throbbing, but I managed to weather the storm unscathed." Her eyes meeting his, she stared into their clear blue for a long moment before she continued. "I'm sorry I ever doubted you, Rider."

"Hey, I'm not worried about it." He matched her grin. "I gather we are free from pursuit and all questions have been answered?"

"Yes. We have been released from your relatives. They got what they wanted, more or less, and we are free to go back to our normal lives. And the feud is over. Our families are friends again, more or less."

His jovial expression slipping away, Rider forced his eyes to the television that hung high on the wall at the foot of the bed. Blinking rapidly, he eventually surmised, "I guess your clients will be happy to have you back."

Shaking her head slowly, a swarm of butterflies danced inside the girl's chest. "You silly man. Are you going to give up that easily?"

"What do you mean?" he asked coyly while remaining fixed on the screen.

Locating the remote, she shut off the set, then demanded, "Rider, look at me."

Cutting his eyes over, he waited, not daring to breathe.

"You told me the other morning before we visited the graveyard that you had grown quite fond of me. Is that true?"

"Yep."

"Good. I've been thinking that building my career in New York was a mistake. I think I'd enjoy the challenge of redesigning flooded out buildings in NOLA, instead. I was hoping I could crash at your place for a few weeks until I can get a place of my own," she informed him without missing a beat.

"My place." He coughed. "You mean in my spare room? Or are you thinking of us sharing a whirlwind romance for a few weeks before you ditch me and move on?"

Unable to hide her joy at his banter, she tossed her brown locks and then pushed them aside as she leaned over him. When the distance between them had been cut in half, she replied in a low voice, "I'm just as scared as you are, Rider Bradshaw. Maybe even more so. My whole world has changed since I met you, and I suddenly can't imagine going back to the life I had."

Rider blinked at her, finding his tongue tied beyond any hope of forming a reply. As if she were aware of his predicament, Merideth slipped her hand beneath his and encased it with the other on top.

"I thought you were the one who was lost, but it turns out that I was," she confessed before raising his fingers to her lips. "I want to watch you sketch and paint…and inspire me…if you'll have me, that is."

Regaining his composure, Rider used his hand to hold her in place and pulled himself even closer to her. "Did you just propose to me?" he demanded with a catch in his voice.

"Propose? No, I didn't propose!" She leapt to her feet, pulling her hand free and stumbling back. "I just meant to say that this is a good time for us…to get to know each other better. I'm at that golden age when I have my whole life ahead of me, and I thought you might like to share in it for a while."

"That sounds like a proposal to me." He cackled, leaning back against his pillow. Raising his hand, he stopped her protests. "It's ok, Meri. Yes, I would love to have you stay with me for a few weeks until you get settled in."

"You would?" She breathed deeply and exhaled loudly in relief. "Wonderful. Oh, I should get back to my mother's room," she gushed, hobbling her way towards the door. "I'll be back in a few hours, though, and we can discuss the particulars."

Watching her flee, Rider laughed out loud to the empty room. Placing his hands behind his head, he found the bandages that covered part of his skull. Feeling them out, he could tell they had shaved off part of his hair. *Man, I must look a mess!* he mused. *But she wants to come and live with me.* She hadn't promised forever, but it was a start.

Pushing the button to lower himself for a nap, the smile remained etched on his lips. *The golden age—that's what she'd called it.* He had to agree it was looking pretty good at the moment.

Thank You

Thank you for sharing in this magical adventure! Please be sure to leave a review and don't miss the next installment of the Unexpected Magic Series ~ Sam

Books in this series include:
> The Binding (book 1)
> The Wicked Awakened (book 2)
> The Secret Sibling (book 3)
> The Whisperer (book 4)
> The Magister's Child (book 5)

Boxed Sets
> The Unexpected Magical Opening Duo (books 1 and 2)

About the Author

Anyone who knows me could tell you, I am a friendly kind of person, never met a stranger and take up conversations anywhere at any time. I work hard, and my mind never seems to shut down, as I wake up often in the middle of the night with ideas pouring out and demanding to be dealt with. Of course that means much of my books were written in the middle of the night.

I grew up and still live in the great state of Texas where everything is bigger, where we have warm weather and a central location. I love my state, my town, and my family, which includes my four sons, my significant other, and many friends as well.

I have thoroughly enjoyed writing this story and hope that you will love reading it just as much. And of course, there will be many more adventures to come.

You can follow Samantha Jacobey at:
Website: www.SamJacobey.com
Facebook: https://www.facebook.com/SamJacobey
Twitter: https://twitter.com/SamJacobey

http://www.amazon.com/-/e/B00GEB5LX0

A New Life Series – an epic adventure, TORI FARRELL's life IS one wild story... escaped from a biker gang and running from drug lords... used by the FBI and hoping to protect her present from her past... IT'S DARK - IT'S BRUTAL, and it's WORTH EVERY MINUTE OF IT!! (Mature read, 18+ for graphic sexual content and violence, including rape)

Irrevocable Series – Armageddon through the eyes of an entitled seventeen-year-old, BAILEY DEWITT's life has become a broken mess... after her parents died unexpectedly, she didn't think it could get any worse. But when the arrogance of man catches up and puts the entire world into a dooms-day spiral, there will be only one place she can run to - the one place she wanted desperately to escape. Can she and Caleb build a life together when the world is falling apart? (New Adult)

Teach Me to Prey – in this standalone thriller, JASON TRUITT and his friends have gotten their way for years. Deceit, sex, and foul play aren't normally covered in the curriculum, but they're doing whatever it takes to get under BECKY STEWART's skin. When one of the boys turns up dead, it's a race against time to save the others; a STUNNING STORY that will get your heart racing and leave you breathless by the end... (New Adult)

Sweet Christmas Series - Life isn't always sweet, even for girls called Candy. Candice Parker's life has never been easy. Plagued by losses and setbacks, each day is a struggle for the petite brunette and her young son. When fireman Gary enters her world, he is one mistake she refuses to make; but after tragedy strikes, she may not have a choice. (New Adult)

Also From The Lavish Family

Fairfield Corners Series

L.A. Remenicky

http://myBook.to/FairfieldCorners

Small town romance with a paranormal twist! Each in standalone style, read and enjoy any order, any number!

Saving Cassie – Book 1: Some secrets are too dangerous to keep.

After ten years in the big city, Cassie Holt is back in Fairfield Corners. She may look like the same girl who left home a decade before but she's hiding a dark truth from everyone. When her life is threatened by the demons of her past, her best friend—who happens to be the local sheriff—offers his help.

Deputy Logan Miller has been burned by love. He's not looking to get involved but duty calls when the sheriff tasks him with Cassie's protection. Thrown into close quarters with the gorgeous bookseller, sparks fly. Logan is drawn to Cassie, but it's hard to get close to someone who keeps themselves guarded all the time.

To keep Cassie safe, Logan must open his heart but that's something he swore he'd never do.

Ragan's Song – Book 2: One look into his eyes told her she was in trouble – again!

Ragan returned home to celebrate her parent's anniversary hoping they would forgive her the secrets she's kept from them over the last few years. When she discovered that Adam was still living in Fairfield Corners she hoped her secrets were safe, secrets that drove her away three years, secrets that could change both their lives forever.

Adam Bricklin was devastated when Ragan Newlin left town. No note, no email, no text. She was just gone. It has taken three years for Adam to finally move past the heartbreak he suffered when Ragan left town. Now he's moved on and everything was going well until the day Ragan returned to Fairfield Corners. Now the melody that he lost all those years ago is back. It's the same tune he heard that tells him right from wrong—the one that sang Ragan was the one.

Even separation can't silence Adam and Ragan's song, and now that she's back it's time for Adam to decide if he should let the song die or breathe life into it once again.

Where There's Faith – Book 3: A past she can't remember. A love he can't forget.

After losing everything in an accident that he can only blame himself for, Robbie Newlin embraced sobriety and tried to live his life quietly alone at this family's cottage on the lake. Grief being his only ally, Robbie was perfectly content with how he lived until Faith moved into the cottage next door. Now Faith had him questioning whether to keep grieving or to open his broken heart to let love in again.

Faith McMillan had no memory of her life before that day three years ago. The physical scars had faded but the emotional ones were still fresh and raw. Living rent-free seemed like a great way to finish her second book and give her the time to figure out her next move, but then she met the reclusive guy next door and everything changed.

To get past the broken parts, Robbie and Faith must figure out if they want to continue living their lives in solitude or take a chance on finding an ending together.

Behind Blue Eyes Series
Sara J. Bernhardt
http://mybook.to/BehindBlueEyesSeries

A father's desire to save his child presents him with an unthinkable choice that leaves him darker than human, forced to roam through time alone as he searches for the place he belongs.

Adam Gold – Book 1: Fleeing the French invasion of Geneva Switzerland in the 1700s, Adam Gold books passage to America with his family. On the ship, Adam's daughter falls fatally ill. A mysterious man comes to Adam with a way to save his child by turning Adam into something darker than human.

The Medallion – Book 2: Adam Gold, an immortal with sweet eyes of blue, rushes through the centuries on a quest for reason and a thirst for revenge. To cope with his pain and regret, he sleeps away the years and awakes in a new era with a powerful, ancient vampire who sets her sights on him.

Golden Shackles – Book 3: When the ancient queen, Sekhmet snatches up Adam, he is faced with a terrifying decision. To help aid her in her vile plans or dare to stand against her.

Plus 3 more segments!

Between the Trees

Kathy Moczerniak

http://mybook.to/betweenthetrees

A beautiful coming of age with a dark side that one teenager must fight to overcome...

Beyond Kathryn Lucas' first memory of her father's tree lay a dysfunctional path of violence, heartbreak, and secrets within a family severely entrenched in the vicious cycle of abuse. A lifetime of fear drives her from her home, and the teenage girl finds refuge with an aunt and uncle determined to protect their niece.

Distressing flashbacks unravel in Kathryn's fragile mind among the turmoil encircling her as she struggles through adolescence and descends into her pain-ridden past. When the summation of her unsettling memories allows the darkness to overtake her, she becomes desperate to unearth the light.

Inspired by a true story, Kathryn must hold on tightly to those who love her, searching for her place in a world threatening to break her as she fights to overcome life's betrayals before she is deprived of her future.